SECRET OF THE VETTIGS

Jeffery Bell

WESTBOW
PRESS
A DIVISION OF THOMAS NELSON

WestBow Press books may be ordered through booksellers or by contacting:

WestBow Press
A Division of Thomas Nelson
1663 Liberty Drive
Bloomington, IN 47403
www.westbowpress.com
1-(866) 928-1240

Because of the dynamic nature of the Internet, any web addresses or
links contained in this book may have changed since publication and
may no longer be valid. The views expressed in this work are solely those
of the author and do not necessarily reflect the views of the publisher,
and the publisher hereby disclaims any responsibility for them.

Any people depicted in stock imagery provided by Thinkstock are models,
and such images are being used for illustrative purposes only.

Certain stock imagery © Thinkstock.

ISBN: 978-1-4497-1772-8 (sc)

Library of Congress Control Number: 2011929617

Printed in the United States of America

WestBow Press rev. date: 05/24/2011

CHAPTER 1

The event happened during the Feast of Courts, a 30 day period of time that was held for all people to have access to the Emperor. It did not matter whether they were heads of state or just a common person. The Emperor made himself available. Anyone that had a matter of importance to discuss with the Emperor could come. That matter could be a mundane matter to others but to the individual it might have been of great importance, it didn't make any difference to the Emperor as long it was during that 30 day period. This gave individuals a chance. The ambassador of Jubal, was one such individual. Jubal, a planet on the border between the Cabal Union and the Empire, was his concern. The ambassador was a man who read the book of protocols, religiously. He was a man full of integrity, wanting to do things in the right way. So with that he brought a gift with him.

"Sire! Here is some honey I have brought you from my home planet. It is appropriately called Jubal Honey. It is the sweetest in all of the galaxy," the ambassador bragged. Beaming with pride he fanned his hand toward the gift behind him.

"Thank you for the gift. It is a nice gesture. But not necessary," replied the Emperor moving on with the proceedings.

"I know, sire. But you know me. I want to do things in the right way," the ambassador said. "The book of protocols states that this is an appropriate and fine thing to..."

"I know. I know. What is it that you need, ambassador?" Asked the Emperor interrupting, trying to keep things moving.

"There have been marauders cutting off the supply lines to my planet. It has been quite devastating to all of us on Jubal. We need your help," the ambassador desperately spoke.

At this time, the science director came barging in from a side door to speak with the Emperor. The Emperor held up his hand to say, wait a minute to the director having noticed him. The director saw his hand and held his peace, staying where he was.

"We will see what we can do. It may be that we would have to send some battle cruisers. I don't know. We'll investigate the matter," came the reply from the Emperor.

With that the ambassador turned. He noted that the science director looked alarmed. He turned to his secretary and told him of his satisfaction shrugging off the director's look. Then left.

The Emperor motioned for the director to come forth. And the director did just that. "We have a matter we would like to talk with you about, sire," said the director.

"What would that be?" He asked.

"We need to go to your office to look at your view screen, sire," said the director. The event was about to begin.

"Well, lead the way," said the Emperor. "And if it is about some sort of oddball creature you have just discovered...I'll bust you down to janitor." He gave a stern look toward the director remembering another time that something like that had happened. Besides it was getting late and the Emperor was getting tired. The Feast of Courts was just about over, anyway

As they headed towards the Emperor's office. The Emperor pressed the button on his wrist band, which was a communicator, to his secretary. "Get the view screen going," the Emperor said.

As they entered into the office of the Emperor. The waterfall picture on the wall went blank, to show that there was a view screen there. It was one of the marvels that the science directory had placed in his office for easier access to the Emperor.

"What are we about to see?" Asked the Emperor.

"Just watch the screen and you will see, sire," replied the science director.

With that the two watched the screen. There was a scene of a moon amongst the stars, and then a bright and shining light engulfed the moon. Then the moon blew up.

"By the Grand Designer! What have we just witnessed?" Asked the Emperor.

"I am not quite for sure, sire. We need to investigate. Allow us to send the science ship, Discovery, to the scene for that very purpose. If you would, please, sire?" Asked the science director.

"We will do just that. Along with the Discovery we will send two battle cruisers, the Hawk and the Falcon. The Discovery may have a few weapons on it. But, we need to make sure that the Discovery is safe along with its crew," the Emperor said.

The Emperor pressed the button on his wristband again to get his secretary. He spoke into it telling her to get him the admiral. She understood his tone, something was up.

The view screen switched on, to show an elderly Nubian gentleman with salt and pepper hair seated on a chair with a desktop in front of him. "Adm. Nal here, sire," the admiral spoke.

"Have you been apprised of the moon incident?" Asked the Emperor.

"Yes, I have, sire. It looks like a matter of grave importance. What are your orders?" Asked the admiral as he was anticipating the Emperor's thoughts.

"We are sending the science ship, Discovery, with two of the battle cruisers, the Hawk and the Falcon, to the event horizon, space zero," came the reply from the Emperor.

"That is a wise decision," said the admiral humoring him.

"Also, send five more battle cruisers to the planet Jubal to pull double duty. They need to be on standby to aid the Discovery and its entourage, if need be," Emperor Ano All said. "And to protect Jubal from an impending incident at the same time because of its close proximity to space zero." He knew this from the image settings that scrolled by at the bottom of the image on the video he had just seen. With that, the screen went blank. And the admiral began the task of issuing the orders to the fleet. The admiral was contemplating what was going on, but it was all circumstantial he thought at this time. The ships went underway without a hitch. The Discovery and its entourage went where they were supposed to go. While, the other five battle cruisers went to there destination.

The planet Jubal was near space zero. Space zero being on the border brought to mind the opposition of the Cabal

Union's philosophy with that of the Empire, their philosophies being polar opposites. The Empire wanted people to have freedom and understanding. The Cabal Union on the other hand, believed in keeping things in secret. They believed that the only way you could accomplish things was to be selective on the information given to the common person. This may seem to be a simplified explanation, but it really was a complex matter between the two factions. The Cabal Union seemed to have hidden agendas and secret societies all over the place. It was a system that entailed approximately 50 planets loosely governed by these societies. And it seemed to have quite an effect on many people. Even in the empire there were some that had similar beliefs and philosophies as did this 'Union' of planets.

The Empire allowed people to express themselves however they wanted. It established freedom for all, even speech. There was one line of emperors that could not be voted in or out. The emperors were the executive branch of these planets executing the laws and in some cases seeing that the spirit of the law was carried out. They had a belief in the Holy Chronicles and the Grand Designer. In this belief a person had many rights, privileges, and freedoms. There was a holy order, called vettigs that read the Holy Chronicles and studied them. They prayed to the Grand Designer on a daily basis for wisdom in accordance to the Holy Chronicles. And they were the welfare providers to the poor. Many admired their commitment to the people. Many people were led by these clerics of the Grand Designer. This overlapped into the lives of many people, including the Emperor, the elite, and the commoner, the businessman, the working man, and everyone in between. They all believed in the Grand Designer. This is why the Emperor did his best to aid everyone he could. This is also why things went so well in the empire. Even the scientists of the day believed in the Holy Chronicles. They proved a lot of the scriptures via scientific discovery. Even the Cabal Union believed in the Grand Designer. Only they had a different point of view in how to approach the Grand Designer. They thought that the Grand Designer wanted them to speak to him in private more than in public. Yes, all the people in this area of space believed in the Grand Designer. It never came into their thinking that it was any other way.

The head of the Cabal Union was a prime minister instead of an Emperor. He had a cabinet of men and women to aid in his governing of this part of space. The boundaries between the Empire and the Cabal Union were very explicit. There was a treaty between the two governing bodies. If one or the other violated the treaty that could mean war. Neither side wanted such things. It was bad for businesses, as well as governments. War was bad for all. This was one of the few things that the two sides agreed on. But the Cabal Union had an agenda to conquer as many worlds as possible. But the philosophy of the Empire was to annex worlds as they wanted to be annexed. Otherwise, they were considered as friends until they joined the Cabal Union if that was their

desire, then they were acquaintances. As the Emperor thought on these things waiting on the news from the discovery, his secretary stepped in to see if she could go on a break. "Sire, I was wondering if I could go on a break? As long as there are no pressing matters," she said.

"Yes, you may," came the reply from the Emperor. "Just be back in about 30 minutes."

"Yes, sire, I will do that," she told him.

The Emperor's secretary, Ann Rae, was a nice girl with a good family. She had been in the service of the Emperor for 10 years straight from the university. She served him well. Part of that service was her discretion in many matters. She never told anybody anything. This made her indispensable to the Emperor. She wasn't a tell all person. In fact she was proud of the fact that there was nothing to tell, no skeletons.

As the secretary came back to her office to be seated at her desk a voice came over the loudspeaker of her communication panel. "Ms. Rae, we need you to get a hold of the Emperor. There is another matter we need to speak to him about, please," the voice said. It was a familiar voice. It was the voice of the admiral.

"I will get him right away, sir," came the reply.

The secretary pushed the button on her communication panel. "The admiral is on the screen, sire," she said.

Automatically the Emperor spoke out, "put him through."

On the video screen came the image of the admiral. "Sire, I have sent the ships where you wanted them to go. It will take them approximately one day our time to reach space zero, the event horizon. Will there be anything else?" Asked the admiral.

"Not at this time. Just be on call, if need be," replied the Emperor.

"Will do!" Came the reply. "By the way, the real reason for my call, the Nova, will be coming back from their maneuvers soon." Then the screen went blank. The Emperor pressed a button on his desk to bring back the picture of the waterfall where it had been before.

The Emperor was hoping that this was not what he thought it was. He was hoping that the Cabal Union was not testing some new super weapon. He tried to avoid war at all costs. But this would be a violation of their treaty. If this was what was happening. Because space zero was in Empire space.

In the meantime affairs of state had to keep on going. So the next item on the Emperor's agenda was to check in at home with his lovely wife, Kay. He pressed another button on his desk that opened an outside communication line directly to his home. His wife Kay answered, "Hello!"

"Hi, honey, it's me," replied the Emperor.

"Me, who?" She said playfully.

"What do you mean, me, who?" Asked the Emperor. "Who else is calling you honey?"

Kay, the Emperor's wife, began to laugh. "I know who it is. I just have to keep you on your toes. It's a woman thing."

"You, know, I don't like it when you do things like that," The Emperor said, with much conviction in his voice trying not to smile.

"Alright, alright!. I know what you mean. I'm sorry," she said pouting. Then she gave him a big smile.

"I just wanted to check in with you to see if you needed anything. Cause it will be a little bit before I can get there," he said.

"Is there anything wrong? Is there anything I can do?" She asked.

"No, sweetheart. There's nothing you can do," he told her with a little bit of hesitation.

"Honey, I can bring you over some food. And maybe some of that good Solian Tea that you like so much," she said to him with a lot of love in her voice.

"That would be nice, sweetheart," he said with a smile heard in his voice and on his face. His wife could feel his anguish and wanted to console him even though he tried to cover it up.

The Emperor thought he was quite fortunate in his private life to have a wife such as he had. She took good care of his needs, his wants, and his desires. Yes, he had a good life. But his thoughts were, not because he was the emperor but because he had a great family life, a great government that he served, and an even greater God he worshiped. It was a government of the people, by the people, for the people, and full of freedom. He was very fortunate. But some did not understand his way of thinking. They thought he had it made because he was the emperor. His thoughts were to serve and not to be served unlike the pervading thoughts of the day. He wanted the people to know that he was as much like them as they were him. He humbled himself. He worked with his hands. He worked with his mind. He worked with his fellow man. His philosophy was give everyone a chance, and sometimes more than one chance to prove themselves. This is what endeared him to his people and why they were willing to go the extra mile to see things going the right direction for all mankind and the Empire.

The Emperor went to the great hall finding himself being led to the chapel. There, he proceeded inside and began to pray to the Grand Designer for direction. He needed to know what to do next. Not many people knew of his convictions when it came to the Holy Chronicles and the Grand Designer. Not because he was private with his beliefs and feelings, but, because the people were not interested in that part of his life. They wanted to know what he ate, where he slept, what his hobbies were, and even his fashion sense. These were the things that the commoners wanted to know about. But the nobility wanted to know about the decisions of state more than anything else. The nobility were more interested in things of power, law, and the administration of both.

However, there were some from the commoners as well as the nobility that wanted to know about both the personal and the governmental side of the Emperor.

In the Cabal Union the Prime Minister kept most of his personal life out of the public eye, propaganda was more important, hidden agendas, private thoughts, and a philosophy of secretiveness that caused people to wonder what he really was all about. This allowed for him to get things done no matter what. There was a vast difference between him and the Emperor.

As the Discovery and its entourage approached 'space zero' streams of data came in from the various scanning arrays that had been placed throughout the ship. The scientists correlated all of the data to come up with conclusions that they needed. As everything was being put together for the final phase of their discovery , the five battle cruisers approached the planet, Jubal. They immediately started to set up their strategies.

The commander of the battle cruiser squadron, designated as Cruiseron 25, turned to the communication officer. "Make a link between us and the Central Command," he ordered.

"This is the Eagle calling Planetary Central Command," the communication officer said into his microphone on the communication panel in front of him.

"Planetary Command!" Came a voice over the intercom.

"This is task force 25 checking in with Planetary Command," the communication officer said.

"Set up your orbit as you need. There are no other spacecrafts in the area at this time. No space flight plans have been filed with our Central Communications Directory," a female voice of Planetary Command said.

"Thank you for your co-operation," the communication officer of the Eagle said.

"What did they say, Sparks?" The commander asked.

"They said to set up the orbits as we saw fit, commander," Sparks replied. Sparks, the communication officer, whose real name was Shad Rah was one of those very conscientious officers on board ship. He tried to do everything he could not only by the book, but in the right way with the right attitude.

The commander, Phil Ross, was a veteran at things like this. He knew what they were going to face. He had been there when the Emperor had hammered out new amendments in the treaty with the Cabal Union in the early years of his career. That was known as the amendments of Mutual Understanding in the space year of 19.80. The commander had to be on guard duty around the Emperor's home planet, Sol. He had to be ready for anything. Even if it meant to go to battle at a moments notice, when nothing else would do. He had the rank of commodore, a one star with the Imperial Fleet.

He was the right man for the job at this time. The admiral, knew that he had a good man in Commodore Ross. The admiral only hoped that the Emperor knew what he was doing.`

The Emperor was praying in the chapel. When his wife, Kay, came to his office to find him not there. "Where is my husband, Ms. Rae?" She asked.

"I don't know," she replied. "He stepped out and went toward the great Hall is all I do know, your majesty."

"I'll check there. Thank you," She said.

With that she went to the great Hall to see if her husband was there. She looked around and noticed that the door to the chapel was slightly open. She approached the door and looked inside. She noticed that her husband was on his knees praying. She smiled to herself, knowing her husband, was that type of person. He knew his limitations better than anybody else, including her. That was one of the reasons why she was so in love with him. She could count on him to be the same privately as he was publicly. He knew when he needed help. And this was one of those times.

The Emperor stood up from his praying and looked around. He saw his wife smiling at him. He walked over to her and began to speak. "What are you doing here?" He asked.

"I was looking for you," she said. And embraced him.

"I would've been in my office, eventually. You didn't have to come looking for me," he said.

"That's okay, I wanted to see you. You know how I am. I can't keep still when you're around," she said.

"I love you , too," he said.

She then stepped toward him. She put her arms around him and embraced him. She wanted to make him feel safe.

He looked into her eyes to let her know everything was all right. He wanted her to know that he was okay. "I'm alright, sweetheart. I just needed to get direction about a certain matter."

"I know you're okay. But a girl needs to know her man knows that, that he is okay. You would do the same for me," she said.

"You know, I would," he said. Looking deeply into her eyes.

The Emperor and his wife had an excellent marriage. But it wasn't always that way. They

had to work at it. In the beginning, they argued, they got angry, and said things that they should not have to one another just like everyone else. It took a lot of work and help from others to make it work. Their determination and faith was what got them through. This was a lesson that had to be learned through experience and not by somebody telling them. Too many times people talking off the top of their heads try to advise others how to have a good marriage. Which is something that only experience and good counsel can teach them.

"Did you bring the food and the tea?" the Emperor asked.

"Yes I did sweetheart," she said very lovingly to him.

"Well, I am famished. Let's eat," he said. She giggled as they walked hand in hand.

They left the chapel and the great Hall to go to his office, where the food and the drinks were. They were holding hands and she leaned into his shoulder as they walked. The servants watched as they saw their monarchs playing out their romance in front of them. They thought that they were so cute in the little things they did for each other. This was another reason why they were so endearing, not only to them, but to the people at large.

"Ms. Rae, would you like to join us for a bite to eat?" The Emperor asked as they arrived.

"That would be nice, except I've already eaten," she replied. "But if you have something to drink. I'll take that." She knew that the Empress always brought too much.

"Of course come and get it. We're going to eat. Hold all my calls for at least one hour," he told her as she took her glass of tea back to her desk.

As they ate, the Emperor thought it was taking a long time to get the information that they needed. As he looked at the time piece on his desk. He realized it was only a couple of hours that the Discovery had been at space zero. He had pulled an all nighter, again.

On the Discovery scientists were correlating all of the data coming in from the scanning arrays. It seemed that the head scientist on the Discovery, Hal Bond, was taking his own sweet time to come to the conclusions they so desperately needed. But he was meticulous in everything he did, scientists were like that.

Meanwhile, on the planet, Jubal, there was something happening a lot quicker than what was happening on the Discovery. The marauders had shown their hand to the five battle cruisers almost immediately. The battle cruisers won a victory against them to show that they were superior in every way. The supply lines were then restored for Jubal. These supply lines were very vital to the commerce of the planet.

The Prime Minister of the planet, Jubal, sent a communiqué to the ambassador right away. He wanted him to know that everything was okay at home. The ambassador was relieved to hear everything was as planned. He then went about the task of sending a gift of thank you to the Emperor.

Now his thoughts turned to the scene in the great Hall. He wondered what that was about.

CHAPTER 2

While everything else was going on the flag ship of the fleet, the Nova, was engaged in maneuvers. The Nova was a spacecraft carrier, the largest in the fleet. The captain's name was Jay Gos. He was a man always on a mission. His hand to hand combat training on the mysterious planet, Sarepta was a major role in his philosophy. It was a planet that was a part of the Empire, one of the original chartered members when the Empire was first being formed and space travel had become a valid form of travel. The treaty was later to be called the Declaration of World's. There were many amendments to this declaration that followed over the years. The great-grandfather of the Emperor's great-grandfather was the original Emperor at the signing of this monumental pact. Many innovations in technology had been put into place since that time.

"We need to get these maneuvers right. In order to make the Space Fleet Central happy!" the captain barked out.

"We will do our best!" The executive officer exclaimed.

The X0 and the captain had a symbiotic relationship. This made an interesting dynamic between the two, because, the XO, Dar Neil, was a few years older than the captain. His way of doing things, complemented the captain's way even though they different. He had a level head and patience, a great virtue. The captain on the other hand seemed impetuous at times. It made for some interesting times on board ship. But the two had a mutual respect for one another. The captain had the final say so, though.

"Well, Pappy, what do you think?" Asked the captain.

"Well, Sonny, let me tell you, we can shave a few more seconds off our time. We need to give a more brief set of orders. Then it will be perfect," he said.

"I agree with you, Pappy," he replied. "Helmsman, let's do it again." And they began to proceed with the maneuver all over again. Even though the captain seemed impetuous he aired on the side of caution.

He barked out the orders quickly and precisely. It did shave the few seconds that the X0, had proclaimed. It was important, because space was an unyielding entity when it came to human lives. Everyone on board ship, had to play dual roles. Some were policemen, some were firemen,

and at times, even, some had to be in leadership roles from the lowliest enlisted man and beyond. Sometimes, even the passengers on board ships such as these had to take over some of these roles.

The handbook for Central Space Command was very explicit in the roles of everybody in space. These were a part of the uniform code of military justice for the Imperial Fleet. Every one had to be familiar with this book. They were taught from the Imperial Space Academy how to read the book, study the book, and use the book. This culminated out of a need to put order into the military infrastructure of the empire.

The XO was very happy in the results of his declaration. So were the captain and the crew . You could tell by the smile on everyone's face that everything was going just as it had been planned. But, they did it several times more to make it a habit.

"Tell everyone that there will be steaks for their supper tonight," the captain said as a matter of fact. When the habit was formed.

The crew cheered. The helmsman said. "I don't eat meat."

"We'll get you the largest veggie plate around," the captain spoke.

"That would be nice," he said, giggling.

"I want to thank the whole crew for a job well done," the captain announced over the ship's intercom system.

The intercom system on board ship was one of those tools that aided the captain in his daily duties. It was very important to keep communications going between the captain and his crew.

As everyone was eating and having a good time. Little did they know that they would be put in the middle of a fray. Even Capt. Gos could not have understood the ramifications of his actions today. The XO, however, knew that by planning these maneuvers on a periodic basis the crew would be ready at all times. This was a strategy taught to him back at the academy. Even though he was older, he kept up with the new innovations that came out from time to time.

"Thanks, Pappy , for a job well done. I'll give you ice cream with your steak," the captain said impishly. "We'll be heading home now. Helmsman, engage."

With that command, the helmsman laid in the coordinates. They headed home with joy, knowing they had done an excellent job. The captain always fostered a sense of a job well done in everything that he did. This was a philosophy taught to him by his father when he was but a young lad working in the hay fields back home. He came from a family of agriculturalists. He was the first one to actually be in the military for several generations. Being on the farm made one impetuous with all of the livestock, immense space, and down time on one's hands. But he also learned a lot of important lessons of life on that farm. He knew what it was to be hungry, to want things, and to work to achieve his goals. This philosophy, along with the X0's philosophy made for a paradigm of immense proportions. The Emperor was happy with his choice of the command structure of the Nova. He had always maintained that two different types of philosophy within a command structure made for a better command on board his imperial ships. The admiral, the Chief Commander of the space fleet, Arn Nal, was in complete agreement with the Emperor on this matter. It worked. It just worked.

The admiral was admired by the Emperor for having come through the ranks by hard work and determination. He also noted that the admiral kept himself educated in up-to-date. The admiral seem to be several years older than the Emperor. But even the admiral knew that the Emperor was older than him, having served him for many years. Even though he did not show it. The Emperor had a son about the age of the admiral, that would someday take over the empire, and he was looking forward to giving him the reins. But at this time, his son was involved in education, and his own interests. The Emperor was very proud of his adult son and all his accomplishments. Yes, the Emperor had a great family, a family that loved one another. And they truthfully care for each other. He felt very fortunate that he and his wife were genuinely in love.

No one knew the secret to the longevity of the Emperor and his line. That was a well guarded secret kept within the family. The right of succession dictated that only those within the royal family unit knew this secret. The only other ones that knew of the secret was the family cleric, and he wasn't talking. He wasn't talking, because, not only was he considered a part of the royal family he was a part of the royal family. He was the emperor's younger brother. He felt a higher calling by becoming a cleric. Even the Emperor felt that his brother had the higher calling. To serve God was always better than anything, else, the Emperor thought.

The secret to their longevity was the planet, Eden. There was something in the atmosphere, the water, the animals, and the plants. The animals and the plants that inhabited the planet that people ate were a contributing factor to the longevity along with atmospheric phenomenon. Scientists wanted to study Eden, but, it was forbidden. They could use long range scanners on it and nothing else. It had the perfect orbit according to the scans.

All emperors and potential emperors resided on the planet, Eden, for a period of time. It seemed that for every year spent on the planet that 10 years would be added to their lives and made their youthful appearance last longer. Even their health was maintained for the same amount of time as their youthful appearance. The Emperor was approximately 250 years old at this time even though he appeared to be a man in his forties. He had spent a lot of his teen-hood and adult life on Eden. Just as his son was at this time.

That is why the admiral gave way to the emperors wishes so easily at times. He knew that the Emperor had a wisdom beyond the appearance of his years. The admiral was allowed to think for himself in the office that he held. And the admiral did very well at this. But still he hoped that the Emperor knew he was doing the right thing.

There was quite a bit of dynamics happening within the politics of the empire. With all the compromising it was hard to maintain a life of integrity, honesty, truth, and wholesomeness. That is why the Emperor prayed to the Grand Designer for direction and to keep himself knowledgeable about things he did not understand. The Grand Designer always came through with the right help in times like these. You could see that the Emperor worked on his relationship with the Grand Designer on a daily basis. It came out with his handling of situations, his conversation, and his lifestyle. Even with this unnoticed act of praying in the chapel, he was

building his relationship. It was the most important thing he could do, he thought.

The captain of the Nova also, an admirer of the Emperor, noted these things in the various situations he had seen over the years. Even though the captain was young he was astute in such things. So much so, showing why he had the position that he had. Even, He was looking forward to coming home for a few days. After all, he had a girlfriend that he was going to propose to. If, she would have him and he could the courage to do so.

It was the daughter of the admiral that had caught his eye at one of the many formal functions that was held within the palace. She was graceful as graceful as the deer he used to watch out on his father's farm. He saw how she jumped and turned on the dance floor it was such a beautiful sight. He thought himself to be a very fortunate man. He didn't believe in luck, as some of the superstitious people did. He believed that the Grand Designer had designed everyone and everything for a reason. Therefore, a man had good fortune smile upon him when he fell into the Grand Designer's perfect plan. He didn't believe that there was anything else, but the perfect plan. Some try to speak of a permissive plan, but he dismissed that. He believed that it was a choice to either be in the perfect plan or not. And this was the perfect plan for him to be married to this wonderful lady, for all eternity. The lady in question was named Arna after her father.

The communiqué was sent to Central Command filing the space flight plan of the Nova. This was to let the command know their intentions of coming home, and by what course they were coming.

"Helmsman, take her home," commanded the captain of the Nova.

"Captain, I can't wait to get home to see my wife and kids," said the XO.

"I can't wait to get home to my Arna myself," said the captain.

"Well, are you going to ask her this time? Or are you just going to hold off like you always do himming and hawing about the whole thing?" Asked the XO in a rather fatherly fashion.

"Don't tell me what to do," he said in a sheepish way. "I know what I have to do. I don't need you to be my conscience."

"Well, somebody has to be your conscience. You need a little prodding," he said in a matter of fact way to emphasize the point.

"Besides, Captain, you know, you can always come with us on one of our adventures," said Jef Bel. Jef was the chief engineer on board ship. He came from the planet, Sarepta, the

place the where captain had formulated some of his philosophy
. All the people on that planet were very adept in hand to hand
combat. The chief engineer had reached one of the highest
status ever on the planet when it came to this type of thing. It
was through the discipline he learned at his instructors feet,
that made him an excellent engineer. He was one of the best
in the Imperial Fleet. He had written many of the engineering
manuals with the rules and regulations of the day. He, also was
the chief instructor in hand to hand on the ship, one of the
many duties he held. Actually, he had several such command
duties on board ship. He was the third in command.

"Tinker, you know that I don't want to go with you on one
of your adventures," the captain said very seriously. "The last
time I did. I ended up with a headache for two days."

"That wasn't my fault, Captain, you were the one that
wanted to tackle that wild boar in the jungles of Makkah,"
Jef said.

"I know! But you talked me into it," said the captain.

"So, you blame me, huh?" he said. "You didn't have to
listen."

"I sure do blame you. You know how I am. I can't turn
down a challenge," said the captain.

Laughing, "I know you can't. That's why I made the
challenge in the first place," he said.

The captain threw a pen at him. The chief engineer jumped
out of the way not because he was afraid of a pen but he did not
want to give the captain the satisfaction of hitting him with the
pen. The captain laughed as well. He knew the engineer was
right. They got along really well. Another one of those perks
within ranks he thought.

The captain pressed the button on the panel of his chair and spoke these words, "Bridge to sick bay!"

"Sick bay here!" A very female voice said.

"Doc, how did everything go with your exercises in sick bay?" He asked.

"Everything went outrageously well," she said. With a hint of pride in her voice.

"Glad to hear it, doctor. We are heading home at this time. Is there anything we can do for you in the meantime?" The captain asked.

"No, there isn't, sir. My husband and I will just appreciate the time off," she said.

"Captain out!" He said with authority.

Yes, the Nova was heading home. It had been a long haul in space at this time. They had been out to space for several months, according to the the Imperial time zone of the planet, Sol. It would be a welcomed sight to everyone involved, especially, with the families of the crew of the ship. This had been one of the longest times in the ship's history for being out to space. That is, deep space. The Nova had been on many maneuvers before, but needed this training, desperately. They needed to have a wake call with training such as this. It wasn't because they did not know what to do. It was because they just did not do it. You know how it is. When you don't have to do a particular thing you just don't do it. It seems to be easier that way. Yet, you know it can work. That was the thought the captain was thinking as he was paying attention to everything going on on the bridge.

"How is everything going, Helmsman?" The captain asked.

"Everything is going by the books, sir," the helmsman replied.

"Keep her steady on course. Make sure everything is done by the book as you have said," the captain commanded.

The yeoman brought a palm pilot to the captain for his signature on the line indicated on the screen. This was one of those duties that the captain had to do on a periodic basis. This was an Update of the ship's progress and its protocols. One of the checks and balances that was a part of procedure.

"That will be all," the captain said after signing the palm pilot.

The yeoman went his way with the palm pilot. The door to the lift opened up quietly he entered and took it to the deck where his office was. On the way to his office,which was by sick bay, he saw the doctor enter into the corridor. "Hello! Doctor!" The yeoman said.

"Hello! to you, too, Petty Officer," the doctor replied.

The doctor went about her business as she passed the yeoman in the corridor. She was a bit preoccupied, scheduling, in her mind the next few hours until they reached the planet, Sol.

She almost ran over a couple of people in corridor as she was thinking about her husband and what they were going to do during those few hours travel time to home. Her husband, the science officer on board the ship, was in the middle of one of his experiments. They had met during a symposium on medical updates through scientific endeavors. It was one of those whirlwind romances. They fell in love the first time they saw each other. Even with all of their logic it was feelings not brains that had the upper hand. They knew that the Holy Chronicles, must have been right when it said, "it is better for a man to think with his heart than with his mind ." Even though science had nothing to do with the proof of this scripture it still bore out in many situations just like theirs. Their romance was one of those romances that worked, a role model for the captain, as well as the crew. The captain used their romance as an example for his own. This time he was going to do it. He was going to ask his girlfriend to be his wife. Nothing was going to stop him, not even his duty.

Meanwhile back on the planet, Sol, there was a buzz going on about the Nova coming home. The families of those that could not live aboard ship would be waiting in the welcoming area near the landing docks of the space shuttles on the base. It was quite the sight to see all of the banners and red runners set up for the disembarking crew. All of the families were appreciative of everything that the military brass did for this part of their lives.

Even the Admiral, the Chief of Space Operations, was excited this time around. He had figured that Capt.Gos was going to propose to his daughter. He had welcomed him into his home and looked beyond the pigment of his skin because he knew he was a good man that loved his daughter. He also knew that the captain did not have a prejudiced bone in his body. Even in this day and age there was still bigotry. That was one of those things that he thought would be as long

as men and women still wanted to be ignorant and envy was prevalent. For the most part, education had helped a lot in the stamping out of bigotry. Besides, why judge a person by the pigment of their skin it was their character that mattered most. This was all part of a speech given by the Admiral to all of the Empire the early days of his present position. This was the sentiment that had been handed down to him by his ancestors that he put into words for a time such as they were in in that day. It was a monumental speech that kept equal rights alive in the Empire. Civil rights have been going on for several centuries and enlightened men knew that equal rights were as necessary as breathing. And should be taught to all, in order for mankind to thrive.

The admiral's daughter was one of those women that was brought up to think for herself. Not that all women were not brought up that way today. It was that she, especially, was brought up that way given her father's position. And she took to heart her lessons on life in the most serious of ways. But she did have an impish side as the captain of the Nova very well knew. He called her his 'little pixie'. She called him her 'stoic warrior.' They seem to be polar opposites, but were attracted to each other, nonetheless. The admiral used to shake his head every time he saw them together. Because he knew the type of woman his daughter had grown up to be. She was beautiful, intelligent, kind, tender, yet she had a temper that could make grown men cry, but most importantly she knew her own mind. He knew that he did not want to get on her bad side at any time. He resolved to stay out of his daughter's love life. On the other hand, his wife couldn't help but meddle. She always thought that her daughter needed a little coaching, especially, when it came to things pertaining to the romantic affairs of life. Her daughter balked at any effort her mother gave her in this regard. After all, she was her own woman, an adult in her own right. The war between the generations still went on, no matter what era of time it was. Even the Holy Chronicles said as much. And who could tell whether or not, anyone could change this. The Grand Designer had designed it all this way. At least that's what she thought.

She was at the university when she heard the news that the arrival of the Nova was imminent. She was in a rush to finish her studies and get going. She had let many hours fall to the wayside waiting upon the love of her life. If he wasn't going to ask her to marry him this time, she would ask him to marry her. After all, she was an enlightened woman that knew her own mind and what she wanted out of life she thought. And he was it. She knew that she could live on board the ship as the wife of the captain. And that is what she wanted. That is why she took the classes that she did at the University of Sol. She was just two days from graduation and receiving her master's in astrological physics. She would be a good asset for any ship, whether she was married or not. She was an intelligent woman. But she knew that she would be on board the Nova with her captain,'the stoic warrior'.

As the Nova arrived and began its orbit, the shuttle bay was all abuzz with the readying the shuttle crafts to disembark to the surface. There was a dampening field that did not allow for beaming technology such as the translators on board ship. This was a part of the planetary self-defense system. This way they could see anyone trying to wage a siege on the planet with the use of all the scanning arrays that were put into place on the surface along with the ones that were orbiting around the planet. Nothing could get by, the space grid, known as the Planetary Defense Initiative,P. D.I. Everyone in the Imperial fleet knew this. Even those of the Cabal Union knew this. It was no secret to anyone that this system was put up around all planets belonging to the empire. The technology of the day was always shared with fellow planets within the empire. Any new innovation would be shared equally among the planets. This was a part of the Declaration of the World's in the amendments portion of this document. Translators were used to transport people and things when ships approached planets that did not belong to the empire or to the Cabal Union which had a similar technology as the Empire did. Translators beamed people or objects from one place to another by translating them into energy then reassembling them translating them back into a solid mass as they were before the process began at the location desired by the translator engineer.

The Nova, the spacecraft carrier, had several different sized spacecraft on board. There were shuttles, lasers, and blasters. The shuttles were the military personnel carriers, with limited defense capabilities. The lasers were smaller spacecraft that had maneuverability with an on board computer with fire control capabilities and laser weaponry. The blasters, were those spacecraft that could be used in the atmosphere of a planet as well as in space. They not only had the laser cannons, but also, photon blasters that sent torpedo like flashes of energy that blew up on contact with its target. But today the Nova was using the shuttles. There were two types of shuttles, one bringing 40-50 people to the planet. The other type was used for a four man crew or less. It was the first type, that was being used today and they had 10 of these shuttles. The Nova had a complement of 5000 in its crew. In the first wave of shuttles the captain would be disembarking the ship. In the second wave the XO would be disembarking. The chief engineer would be staying on board as the officer in command. He would not be disembarking until either the captain or the XO would come back. Usually, it was the XO that would be staying on board. But this time, the XO opted to disembark first. He had a very special meeting with Home World Security, the intelligence agency of the Empire. They had requested this meeting with him in the hope that they could understand a little bit better about the dynamics between the captain, the Admiral, and the admiral's family.

In the meantime on board the ship, the chief engineer was giving orders to maintain the orbit and to do a maintenance on the ship's systems. He knew this was a good time to be running all of the diagnostics that needed to be ran after such a rigorous training session such as they just had. Diagnostics was one of those necessary things that took a long time and kept the computer busy.

As the shuttle doors opened to allow the crew members inside to disembark. The families were waiting impatiently. They were excited to see their loved ones after such a long time being away from them. The crew felt similarly. They felt like a horse in a stall trying to bust of out their corral wanting to run in the green pastures along the countryside but still hemmed in. The sun was warm, the crowd was sweating, and the band was playing the fanfare that they always played when their native sons were coming home, 'Hail to the Wandering Warrior'.

"Hal! Over here! Over here!" A voice from the crowd shouted.

"I'm coming Dad! I'm coming!" Hal shouted back.

"Sweetheart, am I glad to see you," Joe said. As he began to hug and kiss his wife. She was gushing, crying, and hugging back. And she wasn't the only one as crowds of people were doing the same thing.

The admiral, was there as well to pick up Capt. Gos in his limo. That was one of the perks of being the chief of space operations getting to pick up subordinates as you desired. Not only was he the chief, but he was a part of the nobility. He held the title Baron. Nothing much

came with the title other than a few hundred acres and a large Victorian-style home. This home was one of two homes that the captain called home. The other one was the home of his parents. His dad was a farmer and his mother was a farmer's helper, being his wife. The work was hard but rewarding. Both were proud of their heritage, as was the admiral his.

"Well, Jay, it's been a long time. Hasn't it?" The admiral asked.

"It sure has been a long time," he said. "How is Arna doing?"

"She is doing fine. And so is my wife. And so are your parents. Now with the pleasantries out of the way, we need to talk," the admiral said.

"I know. I know. You want to know what my intentions are as far as your daughter is concerned. Well let me tell you I'm going to ask her to be my wife. If that's a all right with you, sir?" The captain asked poised to hear some opposition.

"That isn't what I was going to talk to you about. But we can start there," he said, staring at him in a way that made the captain uneasy.

The captain was beginning to get on edge looking into that stoic face the admiral had put on. He knew that when he got that face on that he was in trouble. And the admiral knew the captain was squirming like a mountain cat backed into a corner. This gave the admiral much pleasure, to put the screws to the captain. After all, he was dating his daughter. He needed to let him know who the real boss was.

"Well, then, what were we going to talk about, sir?" The captain asked trying to change the subject.

"There has been a new development of grave consequences. I have to show you what it is, rather than explain to you what it is. But I believe the Nova will be of a great help to us in this new development," the admiral said.

"Okay! Let's go," the captain said pondering the mysteriousness of it all. They turned to proceed to the limo and make their way back through the city to the Military Citadel. The Military Citadel was a part of the great palace complex where the joint Chiefs of Staff, held their offices. There were several checkpoints, leading up to the main building of the Citadel. This was the place where the captain did not like to go, but knew that he had to go to at times to do his duty. He didn't like the politics that the brass played in this place. It seemed that too many careers were ruined by these so called 'chiefs', the captain thought, present company excluded.

Too many times he had seen good people act like the wild buffalo of the Terran Plains near his hometown. The buffalo were an endangered species, having been hunted in times past to near extinction. Some conservationists had lobbied for a new law to protect endangered species several centuries ago.

As the admiral and the captain made their way through the maze of corridors the captain pondered about the earlier conversation.. He was quite frustrated about the whole thing. He wondered whether or not, the admiral would give his blessing on the upcoming plans he had in mind, marrying his daughter.

They entered into the sterile environment of the admiral's office. It felt that way because of the cleanliness and structured order that was kept there. "Ms. Roy, get my vid-screen ready in my private office," he commanded. With that command, she began to press a couple of buttons on her desk. She knew what the admiral wanted from an earlier conversation with him.

"What we are about to see will astonish you. But keep in mind that we are on the scene as we speak doing our investigations," the admiral said.

With that, they looked upon the screen to see the scene as the Emperor had seen it two days prior. There was the moon amongst the stars. Then the bright light. Then the moon exploding.

"What was that!" The captain said rather alarmed at what he just saw.

"We are waiting upon the scientists on the Discovery to give us their report," the admiral said. "In the meantime, we have several hours before we get that report. Do to the time it takes for a transmission to be sent from the event horizon, space zero."

"Well then what are we going to do with those hours?" The captain asked with a gleam in his eye.

"My wife and my daughter will kill me if I don't bring you home. You know how they are," the admiral said.

"I know. I know. I would much rather face one of the large mountain cats with a wet noodle in my hand than to face those two, when they get angry," the captain said, chuckling to himself at the thought.

"I'll be out of the office, Ms. Roy. Reroute any calls to my home from the Emperor or the Science Directory. All other calls put on hold," the admiral commanded as he passed her by going into the maze of corridors with the captain in his wake.

Finally, they made it out to the limo and began the drive home. "Now sir, I would like to talk to you about what we were talking about before. I mean, asking for your daughter's hand in marriage," the captain said acting like a love sick school boy.

"Well, you have my blessing. I couldn't think of a better person that had more character than you. And I do mean, character, if you know what I mean," the admiral said, jokingly.

"Now come on, admiral, you know I'm a good catch. But more importantly, so is your daughter," the captain said with a hint of airiness in his voice.

"Sounds like a man in love, to me," said the admiral.

"I am in love. When I think about her, I can't think about anything else. And it's affecting my duties, a little bit," the captain said, in all honesty.

"We can't have that happening now. I need, the commander of the Fleet's flagship to be ready at all times especially, now. So I guess you'll just have to marry my daughter to get you back in the swing of things. Take her with you, please! Get her out of my hair!" The admiral laughed. But he was giving the attitude of a vettig speaking on a Sabbath day's morn behind the laughter. There seemed to be a bit of desperation in his voice on this subject. He had to listen to his daughter's rantings and ravings whenever Jay would leave to go to space and not make a commitment, like it was his fault. He had to follow orders, too. And he couldn't make him ask.

"Well, Sir, I plan to do just that," the captain said conviction.

It seemed, the drive to the admiral's home took longer than the trip home from space to the captain. He was so anxious to pop the question. You could see the impatience on his face. All he could think about in that moment was how his beloved would react to the question. He never seemed to know in matters like these what she was going to do or say. When he told her for the first time he was in love with her she gave him a dramatic pause before she told him that she was in love with him just to make him squirm. It was part of her impish nature. She knew she could turn the screws on her beloved captain like that. And she liked having that type of power. But she utilized that power very gently. Even though she was a girl that liked having her own way she also knew what she wanted in a man, a man that commanded respect, and he did. After all, she was as much in love with him as he was with her. And he knew all this right from the beginning.

As the limo headed up the drive towards the admirals large Victorian home. The captain noticed that the admiral's wife was in the flower garden working. She looked up to rub her brow with her soiled gloved hands to smearing some of the dirt on her forehead and right cheek not meaning to. She saw that it was her husband and that he had a guest with him. She took off her work apron and threw it in the wheelbarrow with her trowel and gloves. She recognized right away the second figure getting out of the back of the limo. He was her future son-in-law, and she knew it. Even if he didn't know it, yet. "Jay, get yourself over here and give me a great big hug and kiss," she commanded him. She was like a second mother to him anyway. When he got to his other home, his mother would say the same thing.

He began to smile as he proceeded over to where the admiral's wife was. "I'm coming! Don't worry, Mom," the captain said like a scolded brat.

She began to laugh at his remark. "Don't get so uppity with me, young man, I'll call your other mother," she said harassing him.

"You're on your own, Son," the admiral said. "There's no way I'm getting between you and your two moms." He giggled to himself.

"You're a smart man, Arn," she said. Then she took both of the men by their elbows with her in the middle and proceeded to the house. The admiral was a very fortunate man and he knew it. So did the captain because he knew that his beloved would look just like her mother when she got to be her mother's age, a beautiful orchid of the rarest kind that seemed to last forever. And that meant that he was a very fortunate man.

As they entered into the beautiful domicile the captain began to feel like he was at home. The only thing he did not see was his beloved,'little pixie'. But he knew that she would be along shortly. Whenever, the Nova, came into port the entirety of the planet knew it. The Information Bureau made sure everyone knew these things. It was a well oiled machine that kept the public informed about many matters. And businesses rolled out the red carpets.

Even though he didn't see her, he still couldn't wait. I guess it was the anticipation that was unsettling him. The admiral's wife, Ann, noticed that very thing and try to comfort him. "Jay, why don't you sit in the the admiral's favorite chair, he won't mind," she said. The admiral looked at her with astonishment. She was giving away one of the few luxuries that he had. A luxury he wanted to keep all to himself. But he dare not argue with her. She could be quite the opponent at times. He would much rather have a boxing match with a bear than argue with her.

"That's okay! I'll sit on the couch and let my aching back, keep throbbing," the admiral said.

"Oh, you'll be just fine, Arn," she said, while batting her hand in the air. "Do you want anything to drink, Jay? I have some good Solian Tea made."

"That would be nice," he said.

As she went to the kitchen to get the tea she asked him, "how long are you here for this time, Jay?"

"I don't know how long I am going to be here, " he said. "That's up to the admiral, here." He wanted to put everything off onto the admiral to deflect any of the bad feelings that might come his way. He was very astute in matters like these.

The admiral took note of this and filed it away for future reference.

"Oh, you know he's not going to send you right back out to do anything. After all, we are at peace with the universe. Don't you know? At least that's what the Information Bureau says," she said frivolously waving her hands in the air.

"I know that we are, sweetheart, but you know, something could happen at any moment now," the admiral said, trying to hide the anguish he felt over the images he saw on the vid screen earlier that day.

He tried not to worry his family on things that they had no control over. He also knew that there were some things that were classified such as this that could not be spoken of, even privately to his family. Those images were still fresh on his mind. The captain on the other hand, had other things on his mind. Even though the images that he saw on the vid screen were some where rolling around in his head. He couldn't think about things like this while thinking about what he was going to say to his beloved. This was probably the hardest thing he had ever done. He would much rather be facing that wild boar with Tinker again than to be here facing what he was about ready to face. It wasn't that marriage was a bad thing. In fact it was a good thing especially, when a man found the right one to be his wife. And this is what the captain found in his 'little pixie'.

As he was thinking on these things. Then the door flew open to and in came the very graceful

'little pixie' herself. He just sat in the chair not moving frozen in the moment. He saw her smile and it zapped all the strength in his body. Yes, he knew he was hooked. Even before this moment in time, came about. The admiral giggled to himself. And her mother beamed like an early summer morn when the sun was a fourth of the way up in a cloudless sky. Both the admiral and his wife knew that this was a private moment. "We are just going into the kitchen," the admiral's wife said. The admiral just sat there. "Come on, honey, let's leave them alone," she said to the admiral.

"You're no fun," the admiral said being a little impish himself.

"You'll be fine," she said as she ushered him into the kitchen.

"I hope you'll be here for a couple of days," Arna said. As she rushed over to sit on his lap to give him a kiss.

As they kissed, the captain finally summoned up all the strength he could to push her away long enough to catch his breath. "I'm not quite for sure how long I'll be here, but you'll be the first to know after me. There's something I need to tell you about…" he said, trailing off trying to think how he would say this.

"What do you mean?" She asked what with a gleam of impishness in her eyes.

As he was himming and hawing fumbling for the right words to say. She gave him another kiss. "Honey! Honey! Give me a chance to say something," he said as he was trying to get her to understand and let him speak.

"Okay, I'll be good," she said pouting. She knew just what buttons to push to throw her captain off guard.

"Well, as you know, there has been something that I've been trying to say for a long time. Here it is. Will you give me the greatest pleasure and become my wife," he said getting down on one knee and looking deep into her eyes with all of the passion of the eternal glory he could muster.

She gave that dramatic pause again that Jay knew so well. She wanted to see her captain sweat, just a little. Then with that impish smile in her eyes. She nodded her head yes. He pulled a box out of his pocket and placed the engagement bracelet that was in it on her wrist. This was a symbol to show everyone that he meant business. Engagement bracelets have been used since the dawn of mankind. The very first man that was written about in the Holy Chronicles gave a similar bracelet to his beloved as a token and a sign of his commitment to her, for the Grand Designer and all to see. This was a tradition that no one wanted to mess with whatsoever. With that, they headed into the kitchen after a deep embrace to show her mom and dad that they were indeed engaged.

As Arna's parents saw the engagement bracelet her mother jumped up from the table, and her father started shaking his head. "Sweetheart, does this mean what I think it means?" Her mother asked.

"Yes, it does, mother," She said with that gleam in her eye.

"We're engaged. And we'd like to start planning the wedding right away," the captain said.

"Well, we'll have to get all of the catalogs together, and any other items necessary to get started with," her mother said.

"Well, son, you really did do it this time didn't you," the admiral said, trying not to be sarcastic.

"Yes, I did just that, sir. And the XO will be happy about this, too. I think he had a pool going as to when I would ask her and he might've won," the captain said looking like a puppy that just made a mess on a new carpet.

Arna turned to slap him on his shoulder. "Don't be such a stick in the mud, honey," she said.

"It's already started. First the henpecking, then...I'm happy. Can't you see?" Jay teased.

She just slapped him again. And went into the other room with her mother. And began talking about the wedding. Then the admiral broke out a bottle of champagne from a wine rack on the counter. "I've been saving this for a special occasion. And I think this constitutes a special occasion. Don't you?" He said. Then he opened the bottle with a pop.

CHAPTER 3

At space zero, the captain of the Discovery was looking at the final report of the investigation. "Is this your conclusion, gentlemen?" The captain asked.

"Yes, sir, it is," Hal Bond, the leader of the small group said standing in front of the captain. The captain was not only a military man, but a scientist in his own right. That is why he had a good understanding of the report. He did not have to have all of the scientific jargon explained to him. He was pretty adept at both military and scientific jargon. That was a part of the specialty that he studied, when he was at the Imperial Fleet Academy. Yes, Hez Kei was the right man for this duty.

"Well, let's get this out on a secured channel," he said to the communications officer.

"It'll be done just as you said, sir," came the reply.

As the report was being sent to the Imperial Fleet Command, the Discovery began wrapping up everything to get under way back to the planet, Sol. It was a meticulous effort to do such things as this. After all, it was a ship of scientists. They wanted to have everything just right, whether they were using the equipment or not. That is not to say that regular military people didn't have the same procedures they had, just more faith in them than the scientific personnel did.

On the planet, Jubal, things were beginning to settle down. The marauders had been foiled, and the planet seem to be getting back into the swing of things. Commerce and the supply lines were back to normal. The five ships remained in orbit, maintaining their vigilance. There were no orders to the contrary. A battle cruiser was a marvelous machine with all of its technological wonders. They had photon blasters, lasers, and supercomputers, as did all of the military ships in the Imperial Fleet. But the weaponry was only part of the marvels. They had the latest innovations in medicine, the culinary arts, and biology at their disposal, as well as a host of other technological marvels.

The Imperial Fleet was not only a machine of technological proportions, but the personnel were some of the finest in the galaxy. This is what made them such a superpower in the galaxy. And this is why the Cabal Union kept their distance. They preferred to use diplomacy and subterfuge. They knew that they could not come at the Empire with a frontal assault. So other methods had to be devised. This made the Union such a dangerous opponent to the Empire. But the diplomats within the empire tried to keep hope alive by holding conferences with the Union's diplomats on a periodic basis. This gave the Emperor and his people a hope. After all they wanted to live in peace with all men as much as possible. But the Cabal Union had other things in mind.

It was amazing how that the Grand Designer had placed in everyone the capacity to be either good or evil. The difference between the two philosophies was, that the Empire believe that there was good in everyone. On the other hand, the Union thought that good was a relative term. This meant that they could do anything as long as it was suitable for the situation. They did not think that they were doing evil. The apologetics of the day was a necessary, thought-provoking ideology that was ever prevalent in the society of the Empire that aided in the prevention of war. The diplomats of the empire were well-versed in this ideology. They utilized it as skillfully as the monks of Sarepta used martial arts.

The Emperor, who was on pins and needles waiting on this report to be sent, was thinking that this had to be some sort of hoax. He always tried to see the good in his fellow men. Even those from the Union. He didn't want the Union to be testing a super weapon, especially, in Imperial space. He wanted the spirit of the treaty to be respected like the letter of the treaty was. And this given from both sides. But in his dealings with the Prime Minister of the Union he knew that the letter of the law seemed to be more important. But the Emporer always tried to get him to see the spirit of the treaty. But a lot of times, the diplomats got in the way. Oh how he wished it could be different, but it wasn't. With all of the technological advances that have been made over the last 10 years, more advances than any other time, the Emperor thought how man had stayed the same in his thinking. He wished that the Grand Designer had designed man to advance in his thinking right along with this technology. Maybe, someday down the road when he was with the Grand Designer in Hallowed Halls he would be told why. Until then, he would just live with the whole thing, as is. And keep trying.

The alarm in the communications center at Central Command on Sol went off. "Sir, we are receiving a transmission from the Discovery at this moment. What should I do?" The communications officer on duty said to his superior, which was standing right behind him.

"Put it on an iPod so that we can take it to the Admiral," came the reply. "Then get a hold of the admiral's office to let them know the report is in. And we are hand delivering it."

Ms. Roy received, the communiqué from the communications center, in regards to the fact that a transmission had been received and was being delivered by courier. In turn, she called the admiral at his home. The admiral flipped the switch on his communicator to see the face of his secretary. "Yes, Ms. Roy, what is it?"

"The report is in, Admiral. I thought you wanted to know," she said.

"That's fine. I'll be in the office within the hour. Have the report on my desk. Five minutes

before that," he commanded.

The screen went off. The admiral had to get himself together, anyway. Jay had gone home to be with his parents and give them the news of his upcoming nuptials. His daughter was still in bed from her head reeling about her impending wedding. Her and her mother had spent half the night discussing the wedding, laughing, joking, and crying as mothers and daughters did at times like these. The admiral had gone to bed early with a headache from the hen fest, he needed to be fresh for the next days agenda. He was wondering what the report said. He was a pragmatist when it came to such things. He would give the captain a little time with his parents before calling him in. After all, he didn't know what the report said. And he wanted to know, and have it fresh in his mind so that he could act appropriately. Not only did he want to call the captain in but he wanted to make sure what he was calling him in for. And he needed to inform the Emperor of its contents anyway. So, the Emperor was first on the agenda.

The long drive back to his office seemed even longer as he pondered what was contained within the report. He hoped just as the Emperor hoped that it wasn't the Union trying to flex its muscles and show the galaxy its hand, a super-weapon. They were good at staging events like that. Surely, they could not have a super-weapon of mass destruction. Like what they saw on that view screen. He did not think that anybody had that type of technology. At least that's what the intelligence reports had indicated.

He got out of the limo and told the driver to have it washed and ready to go to the captain's home to pick him up when he gave the order to do so. The admiral made his way through the maze of corridors again. It seemed to take longer in the maze than it did the drive to the base, that was because of the anxiety he felt thinking about the report.

"Good morning! Admiral," his secretary said.

"Good morning, Ms. Roy," the admiral said, with a look of despair on his face.

Seeing the despair, she wondered what could be in that report. After all, she wasn't privy to what was on the video that sparked this whole chain of events. If she would have known she would have understood.

The admiral proceeded to his desk. He took the iPod and placed it in a cradle plugged in a wire in the appropriate outlet of the iPod. He then pressed a button to the view screen opposite his desk and began to read the report and it said 'This is to let you know, what our conclusions are: 1. We have concluded that there was no new technology used in the destruction of this moon. 2. The bright light that engulfed the moon was a beaming signal to trigger explosive devices placed throughout the moon. 3. The explosive devices were devices similar to our own super photon explosives. 4. So our conclusion is, there isn't a new super weapon of mass destruction. And then there was a bunch of scientific jargon and equations that gave the details of what really happened. The admiral gave a sigh of relief. But he wondered who wanted to give the appearance of such a thing.

"Ms. Roy, get a hold of the Emperor right away," the admiral said with relief in his voice. "And get a hold of Capt. Gos as well."

"Aye! Aye! Sir," his secretary replied.

Now, the investigation was taking a different turn. They would have to find out what was going on, and who wanted to make it seem like there was a new weapon on the horizon. This would be a very delicate situation. But the relief of knowing that there was not a new weapon was a welcomed one.

"Admiral, the Emperor," his secretary told him. He turned to see the image on the view screen.

"Admiral, give me your report," the Emperor said.

"I am pleased to inform you that there is no super-weapon. As we were both thinking," the admiral said.

"So, I guess this means that we will be launching an investigation?" The Emperor asked in anticipation.

"Yes, it means exactly that," the admiral said.

"By all means, you have the liberty to do so. With the full backing of the Empire," the Emperor said, emphasizing the full backing of the empire.

"Thank you, sire," replied the admiral.

The screen went blank and the admiral began to give orders to his secretary to do just that. Start an investigation into these things. He then had her come in to let her know what this was all about. She could not believe her ears, that somebody would he be so brash as to have had the gall to pull such a stunt off. But now she knew what all the tension was about , and she could help with the investigation, which was her pleasure. "How dare somebody put the Empire at risk," she said, beaming daggers with her eyes. The admiral thought that he didn't want to get in her way. She could be like a badger when it came to such things.

The call to the captain's home had gone out directly after Ms. Roy got back to her desk. It didn't take long for the captain to arrive after the call.

Capt. Gos entered the outer office. She looked up from her desk and said, "he's in there." Clinching her fist with her thumb stuck out, pointing the way.

"Capt. Gos, reporting for duty, sir," he said standing at attention and saluting.

"Gos, we are launching an investigation into the event that happened a few days ago. It wasn't a super weapon, as we thought," the admiral said.

"What is it that you want me to do then?" The captain asked without batting an eye.

"Take the Nova to the event horizon, space zero and start there," came the reply.

"Right away," he said hesitating.

"Was there something else?" The admiral asked.

"Well, I was thinking about Arna," the captain said.

"Oh! You'll have to keep me updated on your progress, quicker than you usually do. That way, I won't have to listen to her whine and cry while you are gone. I can keep her informed at least as to where you are, and the possibility of when, you will be back," the admiral said.

"Thank you sir for your understanding," he replied with relief. He wanted his marriage to come off without a hitch. After all, he was trying to be a respectable gentleman in all of these things, even if he did not want to be. If it was left up to him, he would be married right away, then and there, and have over with. Then he could have her come on board ship for their honeymoon. Then he shook his head and said to himself, no way. She would kill me. She wanted her honeymoon to be full of romance, and all those frilly things that women wanted. Things like breakfast in bed, not getting out of bed for hours on end, and those beautiful starry nights of walking along sand covered beaches in the tropics. He knew just the right beach, too.

As he was thinking on these things, he pressed the communication device that was around his neck. This was a direct line to his ship. "This is Capt. Gos calling the Nova," he said with authority.

"Aye! Aye! Captain," came the reply.

"Is this Gar?" The captain asked.

"Yes, it is, sir," Gar Nix, the comm officer said.

"Here are our orders, get everyone together. Senior officers meeting in one hour. Captain out," the captain said. "I'll need a copy of the event horizon sent to the ship right away, sir," as he turned to face the admiral, then he saluted, and was dismissed. He turned and left the office, passing Ms. Roy on his way out, hurriedly.

As he found his way back to the admiral's limo. The admiral's driver was waiting for him. They headed for the landing docks where the shuttles would meet him and any of the remaining crew that had been recalled to the ship. Everyone was getting on board, knowing that their orders had been changed. This was one of those developments that everyone had gotten used to, as a part of the Imperial Fleet. Anyone was subject to a change of orders in a split second.

As the captain was thinking on his way to the ship, where would he start with all that he knew. He would have to get some input from some of his best counselors in the fleet, his senior staff, 'the brain trust' as he called them. They were the best in the Fleet and he knew that. But sometimes the problem was they knew it, too. But, this made for some of the most interesting meetings, at times. That is why the captain enjoyed having impromptu meetings such as this. ' The brain trust' of the ship would be exercising their gifts.

As the rest of the crew was being assembled and brought back to the ship. The captain made

his way to the conference room. They set it up on the ship as per the protocols of the Imperial Fleet for senior staff members. ' The brain trust' was already assembled. The only chair that was empty was the captain's. His was at the head of the table, which was a rounded corner of a triangular shaped surface. The view-screen on the bulkhead was on, and everybody was filled with anxiety as they were anticipating what was going on. The captain could hear the whispers of the different crew members that were assembled there. "What we are about to see will astonish you. But, be assured, we know what it is all about. I'll explain more after we see the video," the captain said opening the meeting. With that they turned to watch the video, the captain called out to the computer as he flipped the switch, to say, "security tape Event Horizon epsilon, delta, one. Play tape."

With that, they saw the same thing as the captain had in the admiral's office. "By the Grand Designer, sir, what is it that we've just seen?" Tinker, the chief engineer asked in astonishment.

"It isn't what you think, gentlemen. The Discovery has gone to investigate this incident. Their conclusions were that this was one of those slight of hand tricks that we have seen in the past perpetrated by the Cabal Union," the captain explained.

"Are we sure that it was the Union? After all, we don't know if they had anything to do with this. Do we?" The X0, said playing the devil's advocate.

"No, we are not quite for sure if it was the Union. That is one of the reasons why we are going to investigate. That's our orders, gentlemen. So, I need you to place the ship on port and starboard duty. That will be all, gentlemen," the captain declared. The meeting was over, and everyone left except for the XO, the chief engineer, the captain, and the science officer.

"Can I get all the data, in regards to the event horizon, sir," the science officer, Commander King requested.

"I'll have Comm Central send all of that to your control panel on the bridge. Will that be satisfactory, Commander," the captain replied.

"That will be fine," the commander replied.

Tinker was looking perplexed over the whole thing. He knew that only a handful of people knew where to place the explosive devices on the moon, to make such a thing look as it did. At least, he knew, who in the Empire had that type of knowledge. He had heard some rumors about a few people in the Cabal Union that had the ability to do this. But, they were only rumors. You never knew what was the truth when it came to dealing with the Union. "Captain, then how are we going to proceed?" Asked Tinker.

The captain thought for a moment before he answered. "We'll just have to go to the event horizon and start there," he replied.

The XO held his comments for later on down the road. He was formulating a plan as how to begin these procedures. He was definitely a cautious man, but he was also a very loyal patriot.

He enjoyed the way of life that the empire had afforded him and many others. He thought it was a good word that the Emperor came up with calling the empire, a monarchracy. They were a monarchy with a twist, because outside of the imperial line, everything else was done in a democratic way. Except for the military. The captain kept saying that the military was a dictatorship, a necessary evil for monarchracy and freedom to flourish. Even in the enlightened age that they lived in.

The Nova was under way. There was no telling how long they would be out to space this time during this investigation. It was a good thing that they had gone through the training that they had just before this all started. The captain was hoping that it would not take long for them to find out what was going on. After all, he was getting married. With little a of oomf in his step, he headed toward the bridge, which was on the same level as the conference room.

On the bridge, every one was in their place and began the rigorous task of breaking orbit and heading to the event horizon. The science officer, Hal, was concentrating on the data on his control panel. He had a covered screen with a viewing window, where he could fix his eyes to watch the data stream across the screen privately. He had a photographic memory, which at times was a curse, and at times it was a blessing. But for the most part it was a blessing to him. But it was an object of much frustration to his wife, Joy King, the chief medical officer on board ship. She alone, had a staff of about 50 with a support staff of another 50, all doctors, nurses, and medical technicians under her purview. She was very meticulous, at her job, as was her husband. Wielding all that responsibility thinking she could debate with anyone, still her husband's potographic-memory made it hard for her to argue with him at times, the curse. But she loved him with all his eccentricities. It seemed like the whole crew genuinely cared for one another as did these two did. The dynamics of the crew took a lot of work and dedication.

As the blast shields on the bridge's windows were open everyone on the bridge could see the stars fly by. The stars seemed like little dashes of light against a back drop of black. It was an awesome sight to the captain, after having spent most of his childhood on the farm. He thought, I did like a warm sun, a blue sky, and a firm foundation under my feet, known as the ground but nothing could top this. If people did not think that there was such a thing as a Grand Designer then they were just nuts. Outerspace was one of those parts of creation, that proved there was a God, named the Grand Designer.

The whistle of the communication device on the captain's chair went off, alerting him to an incoming transmission from within the ship. "Stellar topography, here,Sir," the voice said.

"What did you need, son?" the captain asked.

There was a pause before, the voice began, "do you want us to map any of the stars, along the way, sir?"

"As long as it doesn't hinder our getting where we are going," came the reply. The mapping was essential to the survival of all ships. It was this type of dedicated labor that aided in the navigation of spaceships keeping their crews safe from harm and from getting lost in the vastness of space.

The chief engineer was barking out orders all over the place in engineering. He wanted to make sure everything was in pristine shape. His perfectionism was playing out. This was a part of his discipline. And he made sure that everyone in engineering knew it. But the crew had gotten used to his ways, by this time. They knew what all he was doing was he challenging their gifts. This stretching their limitations. Pressing the envelope a little further.

Petty officer Ran knew all too well that he had better make sure he was doing everything he could to make his transition to this vessel, go smooth. He had just been transferred to the Nova. When the Nova had come into orbit around the planet, Sol. Being the newcomer, he had to play everything by ear. He had been a second-class petty officer for approximately 2 years with a total of 10 years service to the fleet. This was his first spacecraft carrier. Prior to this, he was on board a battle cruiser, in fact, the Eagle. It seemed funny to him that he would be so close to his old ship, yet so far. But, so far he had been doing a good job. He brought the iPod to the chief engineer, to be signed. Just as the yeoman had done with the captain earlier. This made the chief engineer, take note of the young Ran. He filed that away, in his mind for future reference, a conscientious worker.

Meanwhile, the XO was taking his place at the seat beside the captain's chair. This made for better communications between the captain and his executive officer. The XO chair was to the captain's right, and there was a third chair to captain's left. That chair was reserved for the captain's discretion. He usually placed someone there to act as an adviser depending upon the situation. Sometimes it was the doctor, sometimes it was the science officer, and sometimes it was a petty officer. It just depended upon the situation. All bridges of Imperial ships were equipped that way. Anyone in command of a ship had that discretion.

The science officer that was poring over the data and flipped the switch to his communication panel on and said, "Science Officer, to sick bay."

"Sick bay, here!" One of the nurses said.

"Is my wife available?" He asked.

The doctor came over to the comm panel hearing her husband's voice and answered, "What is it that you need, honey?"

"Protocols! Protocols!" He commanded. "Can we get together at the noon hour for a bite to eat?"

Perplexed, she answered, "of course, Commander."

"Why do you sound so perplexed?" He asked being a little perplexed himself.

Without explaining she said,"we always get together for the noon meal," with formality in her voice.

Still perplexed. He was trying to be attentive to her needs, and he assumed she knew that. "Well, I thought it would be nice to ask ,you, for a change," he said.

"Alright, sweetheart. It's a date," she replied nonchalantly. Again he felt provoked, but he let it go.

With that, he shook his head and turned to the captain to give him his report. He used a lot of scientific jargon, words that had no meaning to the captain, but, the captain listened anyway. "Just get to the bottom line. That's all I need," the captain ordered.

"Well, it's like this. They strategically placed photon bombs under the surface of the moon and then sent out a flash pulse to detonate them," he replied as a matter of fact. "Something that we ourselves could have done."

"That was the thinking of the scientists on board the Discovery. But, I'm glad that I have you, checking their findings, just to make sure. I don't care what anybody says, I believe you are the best in your field," the captain said, with a little pride and sarcasm mixed.

Beaming, the science officer oblivious to the Captain's attitude replied, "thank you, sir. I'll try to live up to your expectations."

"You already are. Just don't try to stretch yourself beyond what you are capable of, for everyone's sake. Your wife would kill me if you had a mental breakdown," the captain said laughingly.

The science officer laughed right along with him and went back to his duty station. It was about 10 in the morning. According to the internal clocks of the ship. The ship's time standard coincided with the time standard of the capital city of Sol as was all ships in the fleet. The Emperor thought that that would make for better communications and understanding. Besides, the military needed such standardizations.

After a couple hours at his station. The science officer asked to leave the bridge and was granted leave. He entered the lift that took him to the level of the officer's mess where his wife was waiting on him. She had gotten there just a few minutes before he did. "What would you like to have, sweetheart?" She asked as he seated himself.

"I think I'll start with the breast of a barn bird and some smashed white tubers. And some green pods on the side," he replied.

"You're always a big eater. I think I'll just have a salad with a little bit of the wine dressing," she said. With that, they gave their orders to the Porter.

"What did you think about the meeting we had today?" She asked, her husband trying to make small talk.

"Well, I've taken a look at the data, and I believe that somebody is perpetrating one of the biggest hoaxes, since, they tried to hoodwink the admiral into thinking he had any chance of obtaining the throne," he replied.

"You know, that didn't happen," she said as a matter-of-fact.

"That was the hoax, they tried to make everybody believe that they had convinced him. But, he didn't even know there was somebody out there trying to do that. You see what I mean?" He asked.

"Yes, I do. Every now and then people try to do things like that. You know stir up trouble," she said.

"So that is why we are going to space zero and start our investigation, per the orders of the Emperor via the admiral," he told her.

They stopped their conversation as the food arrived. They were always amazed at the cuisine on board ship. The cooks were more like gourmet chefs than actual cooks. And it was the chief cook that cooked for the officer's mess. He had gone to the culinary arts division of the Imperial Fleet Academy. His credentials were impeccable, another one of those perks for being the flagship of the fleet.

In the meantime, the captain had decided to run another drill to keep everybody on their toes. He didn't know what they were heading into but he wanted to make sure that everyone was ready for the rigors that lie ahead. It was this type of meticulous training that made his ship the best in the fleet. It wasn't just all that technology, but the people utilizing the technology that made this ship the greatest in the fleet. The captain knew that. And all his efforts at honing their skills made them better than the best.

Back on the planet, Sol, the Emperor was relieved that the report was as it was. He dare not try to celebrate at this time, because he knew what lie ahead. He knew that the investigation would take quite a while to complete and that it would lead to the Cabal Union. But he needed the proof. He knew the right people were on the job and he trusted them. He had trusted them many times before. Not only with his own life, and his family's life, but with the empire's life, it's philosophies and ideologies as well as truth, justice, peace, and the right way of doing things. In his mind, people were the most important commodity the empire wielded. He knew that if it wasn't for the people none of this would be worth it. Even though at times he was frustrated by the people, after all, he was only human even though he people thought him not to be being their king. His prayers would be with the Nova and her crew.

As they approached space zero the captain noticed all the debris of the exploded moon. He had never seen such devastation as this. Truthfully, he had never been faced with anything like this, at any time in his career. In fact, none of the crew had ever faced anything like this before. But this is where training and methodology paid off. Even the recent maneuvers had an invaluable effect in keeping everyone alert for what lie ahead.

The captain began to issue the order to begin scanning. Every scanning array was at full capacity. As the beams from the arrays searched the debris forming a perfect sphere around the ship. The data started streaming in to their computer. And different duty stations started recording and interpreting the data. The various personnel that were manning the station's in turn were placing the interpretation on recording devices that for future reference. Later on, everything would

be correlated and placed in a report with the bottom line interpretation attached.

As the XO was thinking about everything that was going on, he wondered what they were did without technology, in times past. But he also knew that when technology did not work it was frustrating. But things like that didn't happen today, at least that was his experience. The one thing that technology could not do was relay the human experience to the world at large. And he sure was glad of that.

"Pappy, we will have a senior staff meeting in the conference room as soon as all of the data it has been correlated and interpreted," the captain said. "How long do you think that will take us?"

"Well, Sonny, I believe that will be approximately 2 hours," came the reply. It was 11:00 hours.

"Alright, then in two hours we'll have our meeting," the captain commanded. "We need to know how we are going to proceed after that."

With that the crew was abuzz getting everything together for that meeting. The machine was set into motion and running as smooth as fine tuned limo. The limo was one of those types of vehicles that transcended time and made life a little more livable. "And make sure all of the lasers and blasters are on standby," the captain command. In the shuttle bays flight crews were preparing the lasers and the blasters for launch. This way, if there was anything that needed attention it could be dealt with at this time.

CHAPTER 4

In the Cabal Union, the Prime Minister was launching his own investigation into this event horizon. His reasoning was, he wondered who had done this thing. He knew that the Union was not ready for a war at this time. If it was one of the secret societies within the Union that had done this thing he wanted to know in order to deal with them as quickly and concisely as possible. Usually when things like this were done he was kept abreast of the situation. But there times that a society jumped before asking. To them asking forgiveness was better than asking for permission. And at times the Union seemed to fall into anarchy because of this. If one of the secret societies was involved he would have to place sanctions on it in order to curtail its actions in the future, a necessary action to keep his power in tact.

The Prime Minister called his secretary into his office and began to dictate a letter, "Dear Admiral, this is to inform you that you are hereby ordered to start an investigation into the devastation that occurred upon Vashti's moon. Also, be advised that the empire is conducting their own investigation at this time. Signed, Al Corr, Prime Minister of the Cabal Union."

"I'll type this up right away sir and get it out in this morning's dispatch," he said.

"That will be fine," the prime minister told Mr. Jons, his secretary.

As the dispatch made it to the admirals desk, he read it. And proceeded to give out his own orders to the appropriate people. Adm. Gar Wood was a highly decorated soldier in the Union 's military service. And when he gave out orders people began jumping and asking how high because of his ruthlessness. He was a man that got things done, and the prime minister placed all his trust in his accomplishing the very orders he was given.

The investigation started with Col. Rod Paar. He began issuing out orders to his staff to make ready one his battle cruiser. He would have readied it himself but he had a few things to do before leaving himself. The Star Blaster was one of the most modern ships in the Union's fleet with all the latest technology available. In the Union the military used army rankings, instead of, Naval ones, until it got past the rank of colonel. This was their way of saying, we are unique to the empire.

The colonel was hoping that it wasn't one of the secret societies that had done this thing. He Believe that the Prime Minister had the same thoughts. As he was looking over the reports that were sent to him via intelligence agencies, he realized that it very well could have been because of the methodology use. The intelligence community of the Union was the best in the galaxy. It was even better than the Empire's. Even the Empire knew this. The problem with the Empire's was when it came to such things, who do you believe in the Union.

The colonel began issuing orders to the Star Blaster to begin takeoff upon his arrival. The battle cruisers within the empire did not maintain orbit, but landed on Union planets. The only time it maintained the orbit was around other worlds not of the Union. Being on planet-side made for better security for the ships in their estimation. Because their battle cruisers, could use their fire control technology, while it was planet-side. And it could also use this technology within a planet's atmosphere as it was leaving the atmosphere going into deeper space. This was one of the beauties of the technology of the day for the Union. The Empire, used blasters, with more maneuverability, the battle cruisers had a wider range of weaponry though.

The blast doors to the Star Blaster's viewing windows were open so everyone on the bridge could see the stars flowing by. The colonel put on a stoic face, but inside was awed with the beauty of deep space. He was the type that did not let anybody see the real person inside, being that he thought showing emotions were a sign of weakness. Unlike the Prime Minister, who used emotions as a way to convey propaganda.

The colonel wondered where this investigation would lead him. It wasn't like any of the societies to keep such a blatant act done in the open as it was, a secret from the Prime Minister. He was very adept at seeing between the lines, and that is why he was the one, the Prime Minister chose to launch this investigation. He thought he would start by observing at a distance, what the Nova was doing. He did not want to have a confrontation at this time. There was no reason to go to war just because he was investigating.

Back on the Nova the captain was engaged with his many duties. His stomach began to rumble, and he realized it was getting to be lunch hour. He spoke to the helmsman and said,

"I'm going to the officers mess to get a bite to eat. Inform me of are any new developments as they arise."

"Aye! Aye! Captain!" The ensign said.

With that he went into the lift and went to the level that the officer's mess was on. As he entered into the mess hall he saw a couple of his subordinates eating and conversing about what was going on throughout the ship. "I hope that the captain knows that everybody is a little on edge, not knowing exactly what is going on?" Lieut. May said.

"I'm sure he does," Lieut. Carr replied.

"Gentlemen, how are you doing today?" The Capt. Asked. In the officers mess they did not stand on ceremony, and call themselves to attention when a superior officer entered. This was a standing order by the Imperial Fleet Command that all officers while eating in the officers mess did not need to stand at attention or call a stand to attention at any time when a superior officer entered the mess.

"We're doing fine, captain," Lieut. Carr replied.

"Porter, I want a soup and sand. If you would, please," the captain ordered.

"Right away, sir," came the reply.

As the captain sat down at his table the chief engineer entered the mess. He had felt the same call as the captain and needed to get some nourishment for his body. "Porter, I want a ground barn-bird sandwich and a plate of fried tubers with cheese on top of the tubers. And I need that right away, please," he said and went over to the captain's table to take his seat there. "Is that all you're having, captain?"

"Why of course. I'm not one of those Taz hogs, you know. Why, what did you order?" The captain asked.

"You'll see," the chief engineer replied.

"I know we are on schedule, but I wished that we could be a little quicker about everything," the captain said with anxiety.

The chief engineer studied the captain's face to see if he could understand what he was saying in a clearer way. "You didn't, did you?" He asked with his mouth plopped open.

"What do you mean?" He asked.

"You, asked her to marry you, didn't, you?" Tinker asked.

Now it was the captain that was studying the chief engineer's face. He hoped that he was happy with all this. "Yes, I did just that. And she said yes," the captain said, smiling.

"I'm happy for you. I really am. Did you think she would say anything else?" He asked.

"I didn't even think about that. I was so sure that she would say yes that 'no' didn't even enter into my mind," he said thoughtfully, relieved that his friend approved.

"Well, I'm glad she did, for all of our sakes," Tinker said teasing.

They both began to laugh. The two lieutenants at the other table just looked at each other in astonishment. They had never heard the captain laugh before. To them he was one of these by the book, do what I say, serious officers. They had never seen this side of the captain before, his jovial side. "The captain, here has just asked his girlfriend to marry him!" Tinker shouted. "So, everyone come over here and shake his hand. He finally did right thing for a change!"

"Congratulations, captain," the two lieutenants said as they shook his hand, one right after the other.

The captain thanked the two men, smiling like a lopped eared wild dog. He felt sort of embarrassed, yet good, real good inside. He knew he had the right one. "Well, captain, I know you have the right one, because you're a little more tolerable these days," Tinker teased.

The captain began to laugh, knowing his friend and confidant was on his side. But the duties at hand were still fresh in his mind. It was time to go to the conference room for that meeting. Again, the table was all set in the conference room and everyone but the captain and chief engineer were in their place. The two of them entered in simultaneously, because they had been in

the officer's mess together and took their places, respectively. "What have we learned so far, gentlemen?" The captain asked. The different officers around the table began to look at their electronic notebooks, where they had stored their reports.

"We analyzed the tape to see what direction the flash pulse came from. And we have the coordinates that we are putting up, on the big screen, at this time," the XO was the first to report.

Other reports with their data was placed on the big screen. The computer correlated all data and brought the bottom line into play. The captain noted that the flash pulse did not come from the direction of the Cabal Union border. He was wondering if the people that perpetrated this were even from the Cabal Union, at all. Maybe the X0 in playing the devil's advocate was right. If it wasn't the Union, then, who was it? And everyone else, around the table had the same thought.

It was the doctor that spoke up to break the silence, "well, if it wasn't the Union, then who was it?" Giving voice to the question on everybody's mind.

"That's what our job is, to find out," the captain said as a matter of fact.

This made everybody anxious. "Remember everybody we must be cautious about what we are doing. We can't let our imaginations rule us," Science Officer King said bringing reason to bare. Everyone shook their heads in agreement. They could always count on the science officer to be the pragmatist.

The meeting adjourned. And everyone went back to their duty stations. In the corridor, the doctor and her husband began to speak to one another. "I've been looking over your schedule, sweetheart, and I have scheduled myself to get off the same hours that you do," the doctor said.

"That's all right with me," he said.

"It had better be, Mister," she told him in the threatening way that wives tell their husbands things, when they want to emphasize their position. He just smiled at her and gave her a kiss. She swooned. And they walked to the lift hand in hand.

The captain and the XO went back to the bridge. And then the Chief engineer had all of the data transferred, about this event, on the computer's hard drive to his notebook for better security. This would make it easier for them to access any data that they needed for whatever lie ahead without tying up the computer needlessly. Then, the chief engineer, headed back to engineering.

In stellar topography Ensign Tay was noting an anomaly, with his instruments. As he extrapolated the data from the computer he had come up with the conclusion that there was another ship heading in close proximity to the Nova's course. It was on a parallel course, not an intercepting one. He noted the time and date in his log. And didn't think anything of it, Because in that part of space there were many such anomalies like this because the many trade routes. Because of this being a regular occurrence, he shrugged it off.

On the bridge the communications officer, Lieut. Cmdr. Rahm was listening to space

frequencies, checking for other ships in the area. The science officer was looking over his instruments trying to detect particle streams that were signatures of various ships that could be in the vicinity. "Detecting a ship, Sir," the science officer said.

"One of ours? Or one of the theirs?" The captain asked.

"Neither one. This is a new type of signature. But it is coming from a ship," came the reply with confidence.

"See if we can hale the ship," the captain commanded.

The communications officer began the task commanded. "No one answers our hales, sir," the Comm officer said.

"Try again!" The captain commanded with a little more urgency in his voice.

"Trying. No answer. Trying again. No answer, again," the Comm officer replied.

"Red alert! Force fields, up! Blast doors shut! View screen on!" The captain commanded. With that, the lights throughout the ship blinked on and off and a siren sounded, alerting everyone to the general quarters, that was issued. Everyone scrambled to their duty stations, including those that were trying to get some sleep on their time off from the port and starboard duty that they were on.

"Let's just be cautious at this time. Just be alert we don't want to get caught off guard," the XO ordered.

"Let's see if they are hostile. Adjust course by 3° starboard and 2° upward," the captain commanded thinking three dimensionally. Then the ship moved in the direction commanded. It was a maneuver done with ease, so as not to throw anyone on the floor. It also would indicate whether or not the other ship was trying to intercept or follow.

"The other ship is turning to mirror our course," said the helmsman.

"Okay, gentlemen, we will assume that they are at least not hostile, at this time. Stand down from red alert. Go to modified yellow alert," the captain commanded. In a modified yellow alert, those that left their beds could go back to their beds. Those that were not in a sleeping mode stage stayed where they were until there was a stand down order issued. The rotation of the duty was at this point in time, eat, sleep, and back to duty, and nothing else. This was a modified port and starboard duty. Even though you could cut the anticipation in the air with the sword. Everyone remained relatively calm. They had been at general quarters before, during maneuvers, and they knew procedures. The captain was pleased with the crew and the ship's morale. Everything was going according to plan.

"If, that other ship is on a mirror course shouldn't we try to find out who it is? Or at the very least, where it came from?" Lieut. Roe, the navigator asked.

"As long as they parallel us, and cause us no trouble, leave them alone," the captain ordered.

Besides how could they get that answer as things were going at this point in time he thought. No one was answering their hales. And it was a new signature, one they hadn't seen before.

The navigator shrugged. Then turned back to his duty station. The helmsman was assured that the captain was right. He had been his commanding officer for about five years, and he pretty much knew how he was, and he was the best captain in the fleet he thought.

The captain's thoughts were starting to drift back to the planet, Sol, to his bride-to-be. He hoped that she was faring better than him.

Back home, the fair Arna, was feeling her own frustrations. It seemed that her mother and her mother-in-law-to-be were taking over all her wedding plans. She was furious about the whole thing. So, she went to see her father at his office.

She entered the office and began sobbing. Her father was so taken aback that he came from behind his desk to console her. "Now, now, honey, it can't be all that bad. Can it?" He asked.

"You, don't understand. I wanted everything to be perfect. I love him so much. And I know him so well. And you know..." she said, trailing off sobbing into her hands babbling.

"What do you want me to do. Talk to your mother?" He asked.

"Could you? I don't mean to be a pest about the whole thing. But, it is MY wedding," she said.

"Okay. I'll do just that. Now dry those pretty golden eyes of yours," he said, handing her a handkerchief from his pocket. She blew her nose soiling the handkerchief and all. The admiral giggled to himself. "What have I gotten myself into now," he said out loud to himself. He thought his wife is going to kill him if he interfered. But, he loved his little girl. She tried to give him back the handkerchief. He refused to take it and told her to keep it.

While all this was going on, back at the Nova, a new development was arising. One of the conduit manifolds to the star drive had sprung a leak. Both steam and radiation was being emitted into the ship's, atmosphere. The crew responded immediately. A containment force field automatically clicked on around the emission. This was one of those emergency precautions that the computer had control over being faster than human reasoning and reflexes. It was this type of procedure that saved lives. Once the energy plasma running through the conduit was rerouted the conduit, emitting the energy plasma into the atmosphere, could be fixed. Star drives were tricky. Things like this could happen at a moments notice, that is why the crew had to be on alert. Procedures were very important. Training was a constant necessity. Tinker knew that he had an excellent crew under him.

The ship that was on a parallel course with the Nova was watching the Nova go through her maneuvers. The ship kept remarkably quiet. And mirrored every maneuver that the Nova made.

This made the captain, a little uneasy to know that there was a ship that had similar capabilities in maneuvering as the Nova.

The Star Blaster had made it to space zero missing the Nova by about 45 minutes. They began to do their own scan of the area. The science officer on board the Star Blaster was also the X0 of the ship. It was the belief of the Cabal Union's High Space Command that all officers hold two different positions at the same time except for, captains. Like the science officer and the medical officer were one in the same on board Union ships. Having similar disciplines both being scientific. "Colonel, I'm seeing a different signature with the photon blasts than ours, or the Empire's," said Bar Stow, the XO.

"Is that so a new signature then?" The colonel asked.

"Yes, sir. It's a different signature altogether. I haven't seen anything like this before," replied the XO.

"Science Officer Ray Ess, what are your conclusions?" Asked the colonel.

"I, concur," said Ray. "It is something different all right. Something that has never been recorded before."

"It seems that we have a new player in the mix, gentlemen," the colonel said, as a matter of fact. Everyone on the bridge was puzzled. Who or what could be this new faction in the galaxy?

Would they be friend or would they foe? If they would not be a friend, what kind of foe would they be? The colonel would be hoping that they would be on their side against the empire. At the very least, they would be against the empire, he hoped.

"Keep scanning to see if we can find any other anomalies, gentlemen," the colonel commanded. It seemed like space was getting bigger and bigger. With this new information on the horizon the Star Blaster started down the same path that the Nova took following her ion emissions.

The Nova was starting to see that the trail was leading them away from the borders of the Empire and the Union. They were heading into a different part of space, a space that they had never been in before. The captain was wondering what they were going to run into in this part of space. He could feel the morale of the ship. The thoughts of, what are we doing here became prevalent to him. "XO, give the order to stand down from modified yellow alert. Go to regular yellow alert," the captain commanded. The XO issued the order. Then the captain commanded, "XO, you need to take some time to yourself. Get a bite to eat. And then get some rest, that's an order."

"By your leave, sir," the XO replied saluting him. The captain just gave a hand gesture in response. He was trying to get rid of the XO for his own sake. He saw that he was exhausted by all the that had happened. On the other hand, the captain felt charged. He couldn't sleep if he wanted to. He had too much on his mind.

Back in engineering Tinker was getting ready to retire himself. He turned to Lieut. May to tell him he was leaving. "I'm going to get a bite to eat. And then a little shut eye. Then I'll come back to relieve you," he told him droopy eyed.

"I'll keep everything running smoothly. If I have any trouble, I know your number," he said teasingly.

"Okay, that'll be, just fine," he said. He was too tired to argue.

He headed toward the lift that would take him to the officer's mess level. As he entered the officer's mess, he noticed, that the X0 was already eating. He ordered his food and sat down with the X0. They both sat there exhausted. The chief engineer's food came out quickly. He began to eat, in his sleep, at least that's the way it appeared to be. The XO had to shake him to keep from poking himself in the eye with his fork. After all, they had to look out for one another.

The Porter walked over to the table and said, "I'm leaving now. But everything is out just in case somebody needs something. The coffee urn is on and will shut off automatically when nobody is present. Make sure to lock up when you leave," he said, laughing as he left. The XO laughed right along with him, knowing that they didn't lock up the officer's mess anyway. Who was going to steal from the officers. The whole ship was served the same type of food. The officers didn't get any special treatment when it came to this, and rightly, so.

Meanwhile, the ensign in stellar topography, remembered his report. And he called the captain, in regards to this report. "Captain, Ensign Tay, reporting," he said.

"Ensign, report," the captain commanded.

"I just remembered, Sir, that I noticed on one of my arrays. I noticed..." he trailed off.

"What is it, Ensign?" The captain asked rather annoyed.

"Well, I noticed an odd ball signature out there," he said. "I am sending you the coordinates as we speak." The captain began looking over the data that came up on the screen built into the arm of his captain's chair. He noticed that it was coordinates near the Nova at space zero. This must be where our mysterious intruder came on the scene, he thought to himself. This was getting curiouser and curiouser. He said to himself. This was a line in a children's book he had read at one time. He always liked that line and used it in times like these, when he felt perplexed. He was wondering if his mysterious companion was friend or foe. Similar to the thoughts of the colonel on the Star Blaster.

The Star Blaster was wondering, what would come up next in their investigation. The colonel called for a senior staff briefing. "Where are we at, gentleman?" He asked.

"We are correlating everything right now. The chief engineer and the science officer are being rather slow with their reports," said the chief yeoman. "What is said is they come forth with their data, I'll have everything ready for you."

The colonel was rather perplexed at the whole situation. He didn't want to play babysitter with grown men. "Gentlemen, I will not tolerate dissension among the ranks," he said, emphasizing dissension. "We have to get this job done and I need your cooperation. And if that does not

happen I'll throw you out one of the airlocks, myself. Is that clear," he said sternly.

"Yes, sir, we understand," the XO was first to say with apprehension. The others shook their head in agreement. And with that the reports were in front of the yeoman, and he began the task of downloading them into the computer. The computer correlated all of the data and brought up on their big-screen its conclusions. The colonel studied the conclusions to formulate a plan of action. Then he began to bark out all the orders necessary to get the ship on its way, paying close attention to the details of the report. "XO, I need you to monitor everything that the communications officer is listening to," he commanded. "Chief, you're going to need to monitor the plasma conduits, closely. We need to make sure we have the capability to go to warp speed in a moments notice. Make sure that all scanners are fully functional. We don't need any surprises, like quantum streams." Everyone around the table shook their head in agreement. Then they left the conference center.

It was going to be rather an interesting investigation taking place from both sides. Everyone was wondering who the new kid on the block was and what his or her agenda might be. Never before in the history of either side, had they come across anything like this. This might mean a galactic war depending upon that new kid's agenda. And they didn't want to think about that. War was so messy and intolerable.

Amazingly, back at Sol, the wedding plans were back on course. Arna was hoping that her 'stoic warrior' was doing fine. She couldn't wait for that special night when they would be man and wife for the first time. She knew that he would be an attentive husband, lover, and friend. When they first started dating the most important thing to them was to be friends, best friends. She had never met anybody like him. He wasn't like the boys at the University. He was a man and he was all man. And very much the gentleman in every situation. She just couldn't wait, so she put together a video of all her exploits in planning the wedding to send to him while he was on duty. Her father, the admiral, was true to his word and kept her apprised of her 'stoic warrior' as much as he could. She knew that after the video was done she could count on her father to send it to her beloved.

In the making of the video, she didn't hide anything. It was almost like one of those romantic comedies, where you see all the frustrations of the bride, as well as all her triumphs gaining her great joy. She thought that her beloved would laugh with her and cry with her at the appropriate times watching the video. At least that's how she romanticized it.

On board the Nova the video arrived. The captain was going to have a special screening with his closest confidants on board ship. These were the XO, the chief engineer, the science officer, and the doctor, his friends. As everyone sat around trading pleasantries with one another. The captain popped in the video to be played out on the big screen in his private quarters. As the video began the scene opened up with his 'little pixie' dancing around. He started to smile really big. This was what the doctor ordered. It really boosted his morale. Then she began to speak to the camera and say, "I love you, darling. I wanted you to be a part of everything. So I made this video so you could be in on everything. First, I went over to my friend's house. You know who I mean Cind Rohr. I asked her to be my matron of honor." With that he saw the scene where she asked her. Everybody began to laugh when they saw the two of them jump up and down and swing each other around. It looked like a couple of giddy schoolgirls the captain thought. The captain was embarrassed. The doctor remembered her own wedding and the matron of honor she

had. Cind was actually going to be Arna's matron of honor, the captain shook his head. Then the video proceeded, everbody laughed, the doctor cried at times, and everyone's morale went through the roof by the time it was over.

"Does she have a sister?" The chief engineer asked being a bachelor himself.

"No she doesn't. But she has a cousin. That's almost as pretty as she is," the captain replied.

The chief engineer asked, "can I meet her?" holding his finger in the air. Then everyone went their way, feeling a little more right with the universe. This was a shot in the arm that the senior

staff needed. This is what it was all about, people, people in love, people having hope, and people having faith in something bigger than themselves. These were among the highest freedoms that a person could ever have. That was what the empire was all about, that, and spreading the message of the Grand Designer.

Still, there was the task at hand, that they had to concern themselves with. Even though, the captain himself was still thinking about his 'little pixie'. The X0, was thinking about what lie ahead. What would they run into, and who was the mysterious stranger on board the other ship? These and other thoughts ran through his head.

The chief engineer, after his comical question about the captain's cousin-in-law hurried about engineering doing what needed to be done. The doctor and her husband, the science officer, went about their duties, respectively.

With everyone back in their place the captain saw that they were heading into a part of space that had never been explored before. He noted in the ship's log that there was a need for future exploration of this portion of space allowing the empire to grow in more ways than one.

CHAPTER 5

The ship's heading took the Nova directly on a course that led them to a mysterious planet. "Take orbit around the planet. Begin scanning for life signs. Send all of the data to my station on the bridge," the captain commanded.

"All data is now being correlated, captain," the science officer said. "It is a class alpha planet, sir,"

"That means that the air is breathable, and that it is conducive toward having life signs, doesn't it?" The captain asked, knowing that the answer would be yes.

Then the captain went about the task of choosing a team to go down to the planet's surface. The team comprised of himself, the science officer, a security officer, and a medical officer, not necessarily the chief doctor on board ship. After making his pick, they headed toward the translation room. The XO reminded him of the danger of the captain going on a mission such as this. The captain noted it and the XO put the notation into the ship's log. But the team remained as was. Then every one made their way to the translation room.

"Stand on the pads, gentlemen," the chief translation officer said. Then everyone took their place.

"Begin, translation," the captain commanded.

They found themselves on the surface rather quickly. They began to look around as their hand-held scanners began operating automatically. "Captain, there is a cavern, not far from here," the security officer said, pointing the way

"Let's go!" The captain commanded.

As they went inside the cave. They tripped some sort of device that started a holographic message. 'Curiouser and curiouser' came that thought again to the captain. What they saw standing in front of them was a very life like person. The captain ran his hand through the person standing in front of him and a disruption in the light spectrum was noted. He smiled to himself and began to listen. "My name is Luus. I am a vettig. I have been stranded on this barren and desolate planet for about a millennium. If you are watching this message, then it means that I have found away of escape. But I wanted to give a warning to others about what a vettig really was. We are not from the human race. The Grand Designer created us to be of a help to mankind. That is why we appear to look like you. We are a spirit, a non-corporeal being of pure energy, a type of directed energy to be used for many purposes..."

"Find the source of that message," the Capt. Commanded as the message continued and sounded garbled in the background because they weren't concentrating on the audible message. They were more interested in finding the source.

"I found it! Sir!" The security officer announced looking at his scanner, then he pointed to where it was.

"Can we stop the message and download it?" The captain asked, while the message was continuing.

As the message continued, the security officer went about to see if it could be done. "Yes, I think I can, but it won't come out as a holographic message anymore. But we will be able to see an image on our view-screen," he said. And he began to download it.

"That'll be fine," came the reply.

The message stopped and was downloaded into the recording part of the scanner. The scanners were a multi-functional device that made things easier for them.

"What does this mean, Captain?" asked the security officer.

"I won't know until we have had a chance to analyze this," as he looked at the scanner. "But keep it under your hat, mister," the captain commanded. There was no need for the captain to say anything else. The security officer knew not to say anything to anyone, it was a part of his training. Then they began to leave the cave to see another device, just outside of the cavern. They scanned and analyzed that as well. All it was was the triggering device that they had not been looking for when they entered. Then they made their way back to the others.

Hal, science officer, was making a few scans of his own for future reference. "Hal, over here!" The captain yelled. "Where's the med tech?"

"Over there, sir," came the reply from the science officer. Then they proceeded to where the med tech was.

The med tech, scanning a plant, said, "this plant is lifeless. Yet, look at how green it is. In fact, it doesn't even register on my scanner," the med-tech looked perplexed. The captain just shrugged. But the tech noted it in the scanner's log for further examination at another time.

The captain pressed the buttons of his communicator that was about his neck. "Petty officer Cahn, 4 to be translated up," the captain commanded. With that, they found themselves back on the same pads they started out at on. Then everyone went to their perspective duty stations.

When the science officer and the captain reached the bridge they called for a senior staff meeting. He also included the security officer that went down with them to the planet. Security officer Jonz was setting up the recording in the conference room per the order of the captain. The captain and the others gathered around the table, as usual. Jonz began to inform everyone of what took place on the planet. Then, he began the message from the beginning as the captain and he saw it while, taking a spot behind the captain. After a few moments, everyone began to express their astonishment. The captain pressed the button to stop the message. "Now! Not everyone at once... recommendations?" The captain asked.

"What does this mean? That all of the clerics are some sort of non-corporeal being?" Tinker asked.

"I'm not for sure," said the captain. "Because I believe that there are human beings among the vettig."

"Then what are we supposed to think?" The doctor asked.

"I'm not quite sure," the captain said.

"Then what are you sure about?" Asked the XO.

As Hal sat thinking, he began to speak out loud his thoughts, "we have to continue on our mission, investigate everything." With that everyone in the room nodded in approval that was the only recommendation anyone could make.

The meeting broke up, leaving more questions than answers. Everyone went back to their duty stations, trying to wrap their heads around what they had just learned. The doctor, who was well-versed in the Holy Chronicles began to think about the 'messengers of light' that were spoken of throughout the Scriptures. Could this be the mysterious vettigs, the messengers of light, the scriptures alluded to, she pondered.

The science officer was intrigued. A being of pure energy, he thought. That would mean he had eternal life. How could that be? People die, all life died. He thought. The scientist in him was coming out. We have made a lot of strides over the years. Yet, this puts everything in a different light. He only knew what he knew, science. He wasn't a religious man but, he was a good man. His beliefs were the same as the general public a belief in a higher power that most called the Grand Designer.

The chief engineer was thinking, how do you stop a being like that. If he is pure energy, you can't kill him. So what do you do to deal with a being like that. The security officer had similar thoughts as the chief engineer. But, whatever was ahead, they would deal with it. The captain knew that what he had to do was, just keep on going and let fate handle the whole thing. The XO began to pray.

Meanwhile, back at the emperor's palace. There was a different feel in the air. The announcement of the admiral's daughter had reached the Empress's ears. She decided that she wanted to give Arna a bridal shower. And she wasn't taking no for an answer. As the ladies of both families and their friends gathered together in the living quarters of the palace, where the Emperor and his family resided. They were all giddy over being there. This was not a formal function, but rather a group of friends and family getting together. The only difference was the setting. Only Arna could have been so fortunate. But the Empress wanted to show her appreciation to the admiral for he had done for the Empire.

"Thank you, thank you, thank you!" Arna said with overwhelming gratitude. She had been around the palace, at times. Especially, for those functions that called for her father to receive medals for his service to the Empire. This was better than watching shooting stars, with her friends. And she liked watching, shooting stars.

"It is my pleasure, dear," the Empress said.

"This is such a spacious place. You have," said Mrs. Gos trying not to cast aspersions on the fact that she was just a commoner.

"It sure is," one of the other guests, said.

"Thank you. Thank you one and all for coming to this auspicious occasion. Today is not my day, but it is Arna's day. So let the festivities begin," the Empress commanded.

They played games. Gave out gifts. Ate the food, which was a gourmet's delight. And most importantly, made Arna the center of attention. Arna was overwhelmed with delight. Not only was she going to marry the love of her life. But here she was, in the palace with the Empress, being treated like a princess. It couldn't get any better than this, she thought. Then the Empress brought out her gift, one of the most beautiful black stallion sculptures ever sculpted. Arna swooned. She was an equestrian at heart.

Back on the Nova and there was a different type of party going on. The mysterious vessel that was mirroring their stood steady on course at a distance with the Nova. Again, bringing the captain to the thought, who are they? The perplexity of this question was only compounded by their quiet demeanor.

The XO and the science officer were going over the message that had been brought up from the surface of the planet that they had just left. It was very enlightening to them. They learned how that the Grand Designer had created the vettigs to not only be watchers and listeners, but to interact with mankind. According to Luus, they were to guide men into all truth. But there were some that wanted to pervert the truth and the guidance. This made them think are we on the right track.

The chief engineer on the other hand began formulating a plan as to how to handle vettigs. He had put down on paper, a beginning schematic of a weapon. That was the only thing he could think of doing. His training, philosophies, and his skills cried out for such a plan as this.

The captain began to formulate a plan of his own. He would try to the best of his ability to use diplomacy, if he came across Luus or any other suspected vettig that the message alluded to. It was the only way to go in his estimation. Even though people thought he was impetuous, deep inside he was a calculator.

On the Star Blaster the colonel had caught up with the Nova. But, he kept his distance. He knew that they were not expected. This came from his experience with Empire ships in the past. He also noted the ship, the one that had been shadowing the Nova. Again, he wondered what the Nova had learned. Because he was 45 minutes behind them and they were heading back into Empire space at this time. He wondered where they had been. But he put it out out of his mind.

The colonel's X0 was looking over the scans himself. He noted that oddball signature was back. Realizing that the ship that was shadowing the Nova was that signature that he had noted back at space zero. "Colonel, I would like to report that the signature at space zero we noted came from that ship."

"Are you trying to tell me that that other vessel out there was the perpetrator of all that devastation we witnessed?" The colonel asked.

"Yes, sir, that is exactly what I'm saying," the XO said as a matter of fact.

"All right, let's pay close attention to the other ship, as well as, the Nova. as we proceed," came the command from the colonel. And they did just that. They trained their scanners on the other ship, as well, just in case they decided to try anything. The Nova was oblivious to the presence of the Star Blaster. The Star Blaster had a tedious task, they knew that anyone that did what they did, in such a secretive way, had to be watched. And the colonel knew that his crew would do just that, if not for anything else for their own survival. Capt. Gos felt he was going down, the only avenue he had. He needed to keep on the alert, knowing that space was relentless. At times like these he wished that he had never left the farm; yet, at times like these, he was glad that he, hence the dilemma. His adrenaline was pumping and his mind was reeling over everything. He never had time to think about his future nuptials or anything back home with everything that was going on at this point in time. This was too much of a mystery, and he needed to keep focused. It was about this time that he realized he needed a little respite. So, with that in mind, he turned to the XO and gave him his chair. And left for a bite to eat and a little shut eye. The XO had just done the same thing earlier it was his turn. The XO began monitoring things having rerouted everything from his duty station to the captain's chair pulling double duty. The view-screen revealed everything he needed to know. It was just about that time that the ship began to shake a little. It was kind of like when the blasters were in the atmosphere of a planet experiencing turbulence from the air streams they encountered. "What was that?" The XO asked as he spoke to the chief engineer over the communications.

"That was a little turbulence," the engineer replied.

"Turbulence? We're in the middle of deep space. And you tell me, turbulence," the XO said, astonishingly.

"I can't explain it, yet. I need to triangulate my scanners and correlate the data. It could be that it was a space anomaly or something," the engineer replied, under great stress. Then he began to do his triangulation and check the data. "I'll get back to you, momentarily," he said.

The XO, shut off the communications. And commanded, "stand down from general quarters." Because the red alert, had sounded, automatically when the turbulence was felt. The captain had heard the stand down orders. And turned around to continue on to his quarters. Because he needed the sleep. He began to dream about the Grand Designer and Luus. In his dream he saw a struggle between the two beings. Then he saw the Grand Designer cast Luus out of his kingdom. Then the captain awoke in a sweat. He got up from the bed and went into the front room of his quarters, where there were some easy chairs and a couch. He sat on the couch and pondered. He went over to the food synthesizer and ordered tea to drink. The hot tea was a welcome sight.

Then he asked for an oat meal raisin cookie, his favorite. He took the cookie and the drink back to the couch and commanded the view-screen to come on. Then he ordered the computer to bring up the Holy Chronicles and ring it up on the view screen. Then he ordered it to peruse it to see if there was anything like his dream written therein. He went into detail about the dream, giving the computer the parameters with which to do its search. The computer began to correlate, and then extrapolate the reference showing it on the screen. The reference gave that Luus was a lesser being than the Grand Designer. It alluded to the fact that he thought himself to be equal with the Grand

Designer. But the reference was wary clear, he was not. The reference also said that the Grand Designer was furious. One of the highest laws, not only in the Holy Scriptures, but written in the hearts of all mankind was that one should never think higher of themselves than they ought. The captain thought everyone knew this. But evidently, this being didn't. This made him wonder about the message that he had watched. And it's validity. The captain thought about his dream. Was it one of those rare type of things he had heard about? He wasn't given much time to think on these things, when he heard the announcement from the bridge that they were right on an intercept course with the planet, Eden. He had not realized that that was where they were heading. Again he thought, curiouser and curiouser. They were just following an ion trail that they had noted back at the mysterious planet.

"XO, Pappy, what's going on up there?" The captain asked.

"We did not realize that we were on a course heading for Eden. But it seems that we are," came the reply from the XO.

Just about that time, the chief engineer interrupted, "that anomaly, sir, was a quantum stream."

"Take note of where it was. We'll go back later on, and scan it," came the command from the XO. The captain overheard the conversation and noted it.

"Tinker, I'm coming to engineering," the captain interrupted, as he was getting dressed, putting on his uniform.

"Aye! Aye! Captain!" Tinker replied.

The captain left his quarters and proceeded to engineering. He passed quite a few of his crew going to and from their duty stations, along the way. Upon arriving in engineering, the captain asked, " show me about that anomaly. I need to see if it coincides with something. Understand?"

Not understanding Tinker just shrugged his shoulders. He pressed the button on the panel to show the holographic image displaying the anomaly. The captain then studied the anomaly and the time elements thereof. It was ten minutes after the turbulence the anomaly caused, that the captain had gone to bed and fell right to sleep. This gave him an idea that this wasn't just a coincidence. He wondered what was up. He looked at the chief engineer questionably. The engineer looked dumbfounded. The captain smiled and left. As he headed back to the lift, he became more and more convinced that he was being directed by a higher power. Because, this had a different feel to it than the norm.

He emerged from the lift onto the bridge and began to demand, "what's been going on? Are we

still on an intercept course with the planet, Eden."

"Yes, we are, sir," the helmsman replied. The XO concurred with a head nod.

The XO relinquished his chair to the captain and resumed his place at his own duty station. The captain was contemplating what to do next. He knew general order 12 stated, 'At no time should any Imperial vessel approach the planet Eden, without first contacting Imperial Space Command'. That in mind, he proceeded to order the communication officer to do just that. "Inform Space Command of our situation. Let them know that our investigation is taking us to Eden. Please, advise us if, there is any other way, to proceed," Then the captain said, "let me know what the reply is, as soon as you get it."

"Sending transmission. Now!" Said the communication officer. "It will take about half an hour to receive a reply, captain."

"That will be fine. Pappy, I need you to go to sick bay and make sure that the doctor realizes that we may be in for quite a battle. Tell her I want her duty roster modified. I will be sending her of few of the security personnel on a rotational basis, coinciding with her own scheduling. Also, tell her that I want her schedule to reflect a modified port and starboard rotation," the captain commanded. The XO knew instinctively that the captain wanted, a very personal touch with these orders. With the orders issued, the XO proceeded post haste. As he arrived at the sick bay, he saw that everyone was busy monitoring the various medical scanners. The scanners were important to the health of the crew. They were internal scanners that monitored the heart rates, the blood pressure, and the adrenaline flow, as well as other body functions of each of the crew members in various duty stations throughout the ship. These internal scanners, however, were not used in private quarters. It wasn't that they were not there, but as a matter of privacy they were not used. The only time these monitors were used was when sick bay was full, and they had to use private quarters for holding sick or injured personnel.

Then the XO issued the orders given to him by the captain. "Doctor, I know that this is rather a short notice. But, I was wondering if there was any way we could put together a little bachelor party for the captain? When this is all over," he asked as a side issue after givine her the captain's orders.

"I think that that would be a good thing. As long as it isn't an 'exploitative' affair," she said.

"What do you take me for, Doc," the XO replied. "A pervert? You know, I don't do things like that." He laughed.

"Just so you know. I'll be watching you," she said as she took her two fingers and pointed them at her eyes and then pointed them back at him. With that, XO left.

On the Star Blaster the colonel was planning a strategy for the mysterious visitors. He wanted everybody on board the ship to be ready for the unfathomable ship they were scanning. Again, he was thinking, what was their agenda? Would they be friendly? Would they be friendly to them or to the Empire? These and other thoughts were running through his head. He didn't have time to think about anybody else's agendas.

Back on the planet, Sol, the admiral was engaged in formulating the reply to the Nova. He had consulted with the Emperor immediately after receiving the communiqué from the Nova. He had his comm-device rigged to record his message and then send it to the Nova when he was ready. "As of 1330 Sol mean time, the following order is issued. You can proceed to the planet Eden and there contact a vettig, named Adama. Do not go to the surface without his authorization. And what ever he authorizes, do to the letter. This is by the order of the Emperor Ano All. No scanners are permitted. And as a side note if this order is not carried out to the letter, you will be held in irons. Is that clear, gentlemen. And tell the captain that he had better get his little derriere back here pronto. His fiancee is about to kill me. She thinks that I am the reason why he is taking so long. But, you need to complete your mission."

"Captain, the communiqué is coming in, the one that we were expecting," the comm-officer said.

"Put it on screen," came the command.

As they listen to the communiqué from Space Command everyone on the bridge laughed at the personal portion of the message. "As you were, everyone," the captain commanded embarrassingly. With that, everyone straightened up and went back to what they were doing. He nodded his head in retrospect.

The XO chuckled and gave the captain a hard time about it. "Pappy, if you want to be my best man. You'll never speak of this again," the captain said..

The XO just shook his head. "I'll do just that," he said, still chuckling, heading to the lift.

"Where do you think you're going, mister?" The captain asked.

"I'm famished. I need to eat. Besides that, I need to get a little shut eye, too," he said, still chuckling.

"Go ahead, traitor," he said whipping his hand in the air.

As the XO entered into the corridor he saw what he could only describe as an apparition. It wasn't quite corporeal. It was more translucent. But there was a shape. He said to himself, he was more tired than he thought. He rubbed his eyes, and the apparition disappeared. He shook his head and said to himself, I need to lay down. But, he went on to the officer's mess first his hunger won out over everything else. As he entered the officer's mess he made sure that he did not order a big meal. He knew that if you ate a heavy meal, just before going to sleep, you could have some outrageous dreams. And the mirage he had just seen, if that what it was, was enough for him. After he ate he went to his bunk, a welcomed sight, and fell into a sound sleep. While he was sleeping he had a very vivid dream. He saw a man standing on a hillside saying, "Come over here! Be attentive unto me! And I will tell you what you need to do!" So vivid was the dream the XO felt the wind on his face. He woke up in a sweat, just as the captain had with his dream. This all was a little bit disconcerting to him. He was perplexed about the whole thing. He showered. He shaved. He clothed himself. Then, went back to his duty station.

"Captain, can we talk?" He asked as he maneuvered through the maze of people on the bridge.

"Is there something wrong?" The captain asked. Concerned for his friend because of the perplexing look upon his face.

"Yes, there is. I had this dream," he said.

"Me, too!" He replied.

"I'll tell you mine, if you'll tell me yours," the XO replied, winking.

"You, start,"the captain said.

"Well, I saw this man on a hilltop and he spoke to me. It was really weird, I felt the wind on my face, just like I was right there and everything," the XO told the captain. And then the captain proceeded to tell him about his dream. As they exchanged notes on the two dreams, they decided to put them both on the back burner for now. The duty at hand was more important at this time. They needed to keep their wits about themselves. After all, they didn't know what they were getting into.

As they approached the planet, Eden, they set up their orbit and began communications as per the orders of the Emperor. "Have you reached this , Adama?" Asked the captain.

"There has been no activity on this channel, yet, sir," the reply came.

"Keep trying," the captain commanded.

CHAPTER 6

Back on the Star Blaster, the colonel was having his own concerns. They, too, had their own problems in engineering. The chief engineer had averted some plasma leaks, himself. The helmsman was having problems with the gyroscope in his navigation array. These malfunctions should not have happened the colonel thought. They found themselves heading toward a planet that was not in their computer's system. Because, they had no intelligence on it. But they knew that the Nova was there do to their scanning of the area. What was this mysterious planet all about? They hoped they could find out. This would be one of many feathers in the cap of the colonel. If he could get the proper intelligence for what was going on he kept scanning. It seemed that at times, they knew more than the crew of the Nova, and at times, they knew less. But as the colonel determined this was too important to the Union. They tried tuning in on the frequency that the Nova was using to no avail. They could have listened to all of their transmissions but something was blocking them. They had a listing of all of the frequencies used by the Empire but they were being blocked, something that they had not counted on. Their intelligence had not informed them of such devices. They wondered if they could get a look at the device or its plans that was causing this interference. It was all a cat and mouse game, a deadly cat and mouse game.

Finally, an answer came to their hale. "Nova, is your captain available?" The voice spoke. As the communications officer listened.

"Captain, I have somebody that wants to speak to you," the officer said. "It is audio, only."

"Put them through," the captain commanded. "This is Capt. Gos of the Imperial Space Ship, Nova, with whom am I speaking?"

"Captain, my name is Adama. And you know that you are violating your orders, don't you?" Adama asked.

"I have informed Imperial Fleet Command. They in turn have given me permission to be here per the orders of the Emperor," he replied.

"That is a different matter altogether then," Adama said. "What exactly were your orders?"

"They were to contact you, sir. You personally. And ask what your recommendations were for us to meet face-to-face," the captain said. "And we were to follow your instructions to the letter." With that he waited for a reply from Adama. Adama kept them at bay for quite some time before he replied. The captain wondering was getting impatient. He wondered what the gentleman down below was thinking.

"Captain, the XO, and your science officer, along with yourself are the only ones allowed to come down at this time. Is that understood?" Adama said.

"Definitely!" The captain replied. Then the three that were named gathered themselves together and headed for the translation room.

Down on the surface Adama was waiting. As the team was re-translated into their corporeal bodies the scene that they witnessed was similar to the scene in the XO's dream. "Captain, that's the man," he said, pointing his finger in the astonishment.

Curiouser and curiouser he thought. "Let's see what he wants," the captain said.

"Come over here! Be attentive unto me! And I will tell you what you need to do!" Adama called out to them. The XO felt déjà vu. With that, they joined Adama. As they got in close proximity he began to speak again, "welcome! I am pleased to meet the three of you." He said as he grabbed each one's hands to shake, a custom of friendliness. They could see the smile on his face and the genuineness about him.

"What was that you were saying?" The XO asked.

"Let's not be rude. I will tell you all in due time," he replied. As he ushered them down the hill toward what appeared to be a very beautiful edifice. As they went inside. There was a table with several chairs around it and what looked like a feast on it. The three then smiled at each other and began the process of interrogating Adama. As the questions were being fired at him, he held up his hands to appease them and said, "I'll answer all your questions, as we sup together. I believe, that that still is the custom in your society, isn't it?"

"Yes, it is. But, we have a mission that we need to proceed with. This is all nice..." the captain said.

"Pleasantries are always in fashion. There is always time for such things," Adama interrupted.

The captain shrugged and looked at his companions to get their reactions. The XO had a look of why not, and began to seat himself. The others followed suit. Then, Adama began the task of passing the food around the table. As they began to fill their plates the science officer began to ask, "you said, on the hillside that you will tell us everything we need to know, correct?"

"Yes, I did," he replied. "Where to begin? Maybe, if your captain would ask me a question."

He smiled.

"Well, we have a recording of a vettig named Luus. We have seen the whole message. And are curious about it," the captain replied.

"Where did you get this recording? Don't tell me. I know it was on the planet, Terran, wasn't it?" He asked.

"I didn't know the name of the planet, but it was a desolate thing. We went to the surface

and entered a cave," the captain continued, "then we tripped some sort of an alarm. Then this holographic image appeared. We found the device that was transmitting the message. Then, we downloaded the message and took it to the ship."

"And is the message in your main computer, now?" Adama asked.

"No. It is not," the science officer said. The science officer was privy to what the chief engineer had done with the message.

"Captain, I perceive that I cannot change what you have seen. I can, however, only explain it. It is not in our purview to change the hearts and minds of people. This is how the Grand Designer designed us all. No one but He can read the hearts and minds of people. And even he has designed it so that he can't change your heart or your mind without your permission," he said, smiling.

"Continue," the captain said after a brief pause.

"Over a few millennia ago the Grand Designer and the vettig in question had an argument. The Grand Designer could not convince this vettig of the errors of his ways. He was then banished from His kingdom," Adama explained. "Then, he was banished to the planet you found your message on. We call it Terran."

"Just like in my dream. And just like the Holy Chronicles, said," the captain chimed in.

"You know your scriptures. As I was saying, then this vettig began to formulate a plan. He thought that he could oust the Grand Designer from off his throne. But, he hasn't done it yet. He does not realize that the Grand Designer is omnipotent, where he is a limited being hence the banishment. My question to you, captain is, if you have a message from him. Where is he?" Adama asked.

"I'm not quite for sure. The message began, if you are seeing this message, I'm not here," he replied. "As far as our instruments were concerned, we could not tell if this were so. All we saw was that the planet was void of any life signs such as mankind. There was flora and fauna on it but, nothing else and that was open to interpretation."

"He might not have shown up on our scanners as human, except..." the science officer said trailing off.

"But, the message alluded to something else.. It said that vettigs were a non-corporeal being, a being of pure energy," the XO finished the science officer's thought.

"Yes! That is right. But it has been a well guarded secret, only known to a handful of humans. I am surprised that Luus spoke of this. Talk of this is forbidden. Yet, I'm not surprised. He wants to upset any of the plans that the Grand Designer has," explained Adama.

Everyone was listening to this explanation and unconsciously eating. They needed a few moments to reflect on what was being said. It takes human beings little more time to understand such things. The captain's thoughts were curiouser and curiouser. The XO's thoughts were, what

next? The science officers thoughts were, how do I explain this one? His scientific nature was screaming in his head. Logic, at least the logic he understood, would not help him this time. He also thought how his wife would be giggling at him, at this time. Then she would say something like 'my prayers have been answered'. And he knew what she meant by that.

Then it was Adama that broke the silence, "gentlemen, I need you to bring that message to me. It is of a vital importance to the cause of truth that that message should not fall into the wrong hands. So, please, do as I ask."

"As soon as we get on board ship. We will comply," replied the captain remembering his orders from the admiral. "We are of the same mind as you. But I have one more question. Are there human's mingled within your ranks?"

"Yes, there are," he replied. "This is so that if this secret was to get out no one could know who was a real vettig and who wasn't, as the message alluded that all vettigs were , as I am."

"And are you human, or the other thing?" The captain asked.

"I'm the other thing as you have put it. This image that you see has been designed to allow us to interact with mankind. But we can shed this image, like, you can your clothing. But it does not behoove us to do so," he replied to the captain with no further explanation.

"Well, if you're the type of being, you are. What type of being is the Grand Designer?" The captain asked. Adama was not forthcoming with the answer. Basically, he did not know, other than what he had already explained.

"Well, gentlemen, we must be heading to the ship. May we return, after we have been debriefed?" Asked the captain.

"Yes, you may. But only you, captain," Adama replied. "And you, XO, are a blessed man, because you can tune into our frequency. And you Hal King congratulations." The science officer was perplexed. What a cryptic message he thought.

They went outside of the edifice the captain pressed the communicator on his neck and commanded, "translate us up, petty officer." And with that, they were translated back up to the ship. When they were back on the ship, they went about the task of getting back to duty. The captain got the 'message' from the chief engineer. After being debriefed by security as protocol dictated. And then, he headed back to the surface. He wanted one more shot at Adama.

On the surface, he approached the edifice that he had eaten in. He wondered what he would find there. As he was looking around he saw a bright light coming from a long hallway that he had not noticed before. Then the light vanished. And out of the hallway came Adama. "Captain, I'm pleased to see you again. Have you got the 'message'?" He asked.

"Right here," the captain said holding up the 'notepad' that had the message on it. "I wanted to ask you something."

"What is it?" He asked with an idea what the captain was about to ask.

"I had a dream and was wondering what it was all about," he queried.

"Had you read the Scriptures that you had dreamed about before or after your arrival at Terran?" He inquired.

"After," came the reply.

"You have been blessed. It was the Grand Designer that infiltrated your dreams. He must be very interested in you to have done such a thing," he told him.

"Can you tell me anything else?" the captain asked.

"Only that, you are blessed," he interrupted his train of thought. "His ways are above your ways and mine as well. Only He knows what must be. My advice to you, would be to begin to study the Holy Chronicles. Starting with the Book of Witnesses in the New Tribute. Do you understand?"

"I believe so," he replied hesitantly. There was a bit of trying to figure all this out in his mind, which reflected on his face. Adama smiled. Then he turned and went back down the hall. The captain dared not follow him. He did not know what he would run into if he did. He then went outside. "Translate me up," he said on his communicator, as he had done so many times before.

Back on the ship, he began to order another senior staff meeting. As he entered into the senior staff room after having called this meeting via the intercom. He started the meeting, "explain what just happened on the surface, XO, to the rest."

"We were on the surface..." he started to say, and then caught himself.

"Go on!" The chief engineer, encouraged.

"And a day before we got here. I had a dream. In that dream was a man that told us to listen to what he had to say," he paraphrased. "And when we got to the surface of the planet. We encountered that very man. It was like déjà vu. I can't explain it, but, it happened."

"And then what?" The doctor inquired.

"He told us all about the vettigs. Just like on the message and then the captain's dream," he said.

"You had a dream, too?" The doctor asked.

"Yes. But let him finish," the captain commanded pointing at the XO.

"Then we ate. And the vettig explained further. He told us about a great struggle in the kingdom of the Grand Designer. And how that the message that we saw from that other planet, a planet called Terran was correct in some of its content. Now, we need to come up with a plan as to what to do about it," the XO said.

"And that's not all," the science officer said. "He gave us each some cryptic messages. To the XO, he said, you are blessed. To me he said, congratulations. Just, congratulations. Go figure."

Everyone laughed at his perplexity. His wife got up and gave him a big kiss and said, "you look like a big baby. It seems to me that this being is a little eccentric."

"With all eccentricities aside, I need your recommendations," said the captain.

As everyone contemplated silently. It was the security officer that spoke up, "well, we need to find this Luus, don't we?" Because he was also included in this conference because of his involvement with the message. "And when we get him, what are we supposed to do with him?"

"We'll get to that, when we cross that bridge if we ever do," the captain said.

The meeting broke up. And everyone went back to their duty stations. The chief engineer went into engineering and relieved his second-in-command there. The captain issued an order to the X0, that he did not want the two of them on the bridge together except for relieving one another or general quarters, which ever the case may be. The doctor went back to sick bay, to relieve her second-in-command as well and fainted. Those that were in close proximity to the doctor were alarmed and went to her side. "Doctor, we need to get you on the gurney. And transfer you over to one of our diagnosis beds," Dr. Arnett, her second-in-command was speaking to her. The doctor was a little groggy, as Dr. Arnett began scanning her body for anomalies after doing just what she said with the gurney and all. She then smiled from ear to ear. "Why, Doctor, you're pregnant!" As the good doctor came out of her fog, she heard the good news.

"Get a hold of my husband! Right away!" She said excitedly.

"Commander King, to the sick bay. On the double!" Dr. Arnett commanded, hiding the real intent of his command as the Chief Medical Officer requested.

The commander ran to the lift thinking something happened with his wife. Otherwise, she would be the one calling him, not Dr. Arnett. Concerned, it didn't take him any time to get there. "What's going on!?" He said with concern border lining on worry.

"Nothing, sweetheart, nothing," she said rather mysteriously.

"Then what is it? Why are you lying there? Are you sick?" He said, as a concerned husband.

"Honey, I'm pregnant! Not sick!" She said, surprising him.

"Honey," he said tenderly, "so this means?"

"Yes," she said, nodding her head, "congratulations! Daddy." Then he remembered what the vettig said back on the surface. How could he have known he wondered.

"This is one of the many prayers I have been praying. It's really happening. We are going to be parents," she said, and then started crying.

"Honey," he said consoling her. He embraced her. He hugged her. And he held her tenderly as did most men in this situation. Everyone in the sick bay, wore smiles at the announcement. All this was happening , and the mission, too. The chief science officer had to sit down being overwhelmed. Then Dr. Arnett began to laugh. "It looks like the daddy is going to faint, like the mommy did," he said teasingly.

While, this was all going on the XO, back in his quarters was getting some much-needed sleep. Then the general quarters sounded. Everyone hopped to their perspective duty stations disturbing his sleep. In the sick bay, the chief science officer was hesitant about leaving. When the doctor said, "go ahead. We'll take good care of her. You're needed on the bridge." With that, he left to go to the bridge. The XO and chief engineer was already on the lift, when the science officer entered into it.

"I'm going to be a daddy," he said the beaming. The XO held his finger up in astonishment. He didn't know what to say.

"Congratulations!" The chief engineer, said remembering what Adama said back on Eden.

"It's what you've been wanting for a long time!" The XO exclaimed. "Then, congratulations," Then he stuck out his hand and shook his friend's hand. "We'll have to tell the captain later," wondering what this general quarters was all about? The chief science officer nodded in agreement.

"Gentlemen, there is a space ship approaching," the captain said as the two emerged from the lift and took their places. Looking on the main screen in front of them. They saw the ship approaching.

"Have you tried to hale them?" The XO asked, obviously knowing the answer.

"Yes, we have," the communication officer replied. "No answer to our hale."

As the science officer was monitoring the scanners. He said, "it has a configuration that I have never seen before."

The captain perplexed, just watched as the whole scene played out. Then all of a sudden the ship just stopped as if it knew that they had been seen. It just sat there for what seemed an eternity. The captain was beginning to sweat. In his mind he was wondering why all of a sudden his shadow revealed itself. "Try haling them again," he commanded. He was oblivious to the fact that more than one ship was shadowing him.

"Sending transmission now. No answer. Sending again. No answer, again. What should we do?" The comm-officer asked.

It was at this time that Adama broke into the communication frequency that the Nova was using to hale the other ship. "Captain, I believe I can explain everything. If you will permit me to do so," Adama said.

"Captain, it's the gentleman from the planet down below. He says he has an explanation for us," the comm-officer said recognizing the voice from before. "This time, my instruments indicate that we have video as well as audio."

"Put him on the screen," commanded the captain.

The screen came on, the captain as well as the rest of the crew saw a muscular man with a white beard and a youthful face similar to what they encountered planet-side. But everyone saw him as a good and gentle person. Instinctively, they knew he had their best interests at heart. Everyone became at ease. "Captain, the persons on that ship are here to see me. And if you will give me a little more of your time here on the surface and bring your lovely chief medical officer. We will explain everything when you get here," Adama said.

"We'll be right there. Capt. Gos, out," he said. Then he turned to comm-officer as he stood up and waved his hand across his neck. The comm-officer pressed a button and the screen went blank.

Orders were issued to the chief medical officer, via the XO to meet the captain at the translation room. The captain was waiting on the pads. When the chief medical officer, was accompanied by her husband, who had met her along the way. "You're not coming," the captain commanded.

"Why not?" The chief science officer asked questioning his authority. He had a scowl on his face.

"It's all right, honey. I feel at ease. I can't explain it. I just do," she said putting his mind at ease. Then he nodded his head in agreement and let her go.

"Begin translation," the captain commanded the petty officer.

As they found themselves on the surface one more time. The doctor was amazed at the edifice being the first time she had seen it. There was a welcoming committee of four, at its entrance . "Captain, Doctor, let me introduce you. These are three of my dearest friends. This is Enosh. This is Abram. And this is Jess," Adama said. As each one held out their hands in friendship.

"Please to me to," the doctor said, smiling at the sight.

"Me, too," the captain said with a little perplexity, in his voice.

"Why am I here?" The doctor asked.

"We'll get to that in a moment. But right now, we need to speak with the captain. You need not concern yourself with anything at this time. Just listen," he said putting the doctor at ease.

"We have been monitoring your progress," said Enosh. "And we must say. So far you have done an excellent job at things."

"Yes, thank you, but gentlemen, why are we here?" The captain inquired.

"Because we felt a disturbance that was not natural in your part of space. And we wanted to investigate what it was. Can you give us a little bit more on this?" Abram injected.

"Well, we witnessed the explosion of a moon. We believed that it was a man-made explosion. And with that, we began an investigation. My ship, and my crew, and I were brought into this situation. And furthermore..." he said.

"Then tell us what are your conclusions," Jess interrupted wanting to get right to the facts.

"Well, so far we have found more questions than answers. We have this message that we have handed over to Adama that could explain a little more of the details than I could at this time. We would like to have your input," the captain requested.

With that the four turned toward one another and began to speak in a huddle in a whisper. Their voices were so low that neither the captain or the doctor could comprehend them. Then they turned to gaze upon the doctor, and it was Jess that began, "you are a blessed vessel. The child that you are carrying will aid in the furthering of the kingdom of the Grand Designer."

"How did you know? By what means did you discover this? What do you mean by furthering the kingdom?" She inquired as one having faith.

"That attitude has been designed in your very being," Abram said trying to skirt the issue. This was a tactic to keep her off guard. Her thoughts turned to her condition, what type of child was she carrying.

"What is this kingdom,that I keep hearing about?" The captain asked inquisitively.

"That is something only answered at the Grand Designer's discretion or by death," explained Adama. With that, the captain just looked at him dumbfounded. "That's all right, Captain. You'll understand someday. Right now it is enough to know that the Grand Designer is on your side. He is a being of absolute power, absolute love, and absolute knowing," Adama explained further.

"And He is everywhere in every time period. It is a little hard to understand. Just accept it. We can give no further explanation than that," Jess said.

"Then by your leave, sirs, we will be going," the captain said nodding his head in a manner of respect.

"By all means, do so," Adama told him. Adama was pleased with the outcome of this meeting. "And we will be sending you some information on how you can find Luus."

"Thank you," the captain said appreciatively.

"And thank you. You have given me a lot to think about. I'll be in much prayer, from this time on," the doctor said.

With that the two turned and left the building. The four that remained inside, went down that mysterious hallway. The captain then, as many times before, called up to his ship to have them translate he and the doctor back on board. There was a lot for them to take in and to mull over. The doctor needed to make the announcement about her child realizing what the vettig's had said. She needed to speak with her husband about all these things. Then she realized, a son. Hal would tickled to hear.

It was evening according to the internal sensors. Remembering everything that was said, she went about fixing up their quarters, to ease her husband into the information, she just received. She was singing and praising the Grand Designer for everything. What kind of being was he? She knew that he was a higher powerbut she didn't realize he was God. In accordance to everything she had learned on the surface, this was so. She had converted what they said into the three "omni's", omni-present, omniscient, omnipotent. This was the only way that she could explain it in terms that her husband could wrap his head around. He needed to have the 7500 credit words directed at him, in order for him to understand. And she knew that. Along with her preparations, she got out a bit of the synthetic champagne. This was a nonalcoholic beverage that she could imbibe. She was dancing around feeling giddy. Her husband came in, perplexed at her attitude. "What's going on?" He asked, thinking she had gone bonkers.

"When I went down to the surface. There were these men, these beings..." she was to giddy to finish her thoughts.

"Have you been drinking?" He asked, watching her seemingly making a fool of herself.

"No! You know that I'm a doctor, and in my condition it would be bad for the baby. Besides, you know, my personal convictions about such things as that. I'm trying to tell you that they told me, we're going to have a son. I can't tell you how they knew, because at this stage in my pregnancy, even with our advanced medical science it's still too early to tell. We have to wait at least four weeks. Then we can take a sample of DNA from the fetus and examine it to declare what sex it is. Part of our design," she told him.

"Well, that's different," he said shaking his head. "Are you telling me that they told you that we're having a boy." He looked at her astonishingly.

"Yes! Yes, yes, yes!" She said, dancing him around the room. They both began to laugh.

"What was the captain's reaction when he heard the news?" He asked her.

"At first he was astonished. Then he smiled. Then he realized why you were acting the way you were on the bridge just before we were whisked away to the surface. He said as much so, when we left the translation room," she replied.

"I bet he thinks I'm nuts," he said whimsically.

"No, he doesn't think that. He thinks you're like the rest of the perspective fathers out there. And he knows, no matter how intelligent you are that emotions can make even, someone like you look like a babbling idiot," she said teasingly.

"Come on now. Give me a break, please," he pleaded. With that she gave him a great big kiss

and began to cry again. "What is it now?"

"I'm just so happy. Everything is right in the galaxy. Right with my husband. Right with everything," she said. Then she remembered, "I need to get a hold of our parents."

She was making his head swim. He thought he was in the middle of cyclone season in the plains of Sarepta on Sol. Things were happening too fast. He didn't know what to do. And he was the intelligent one. He just wanted to keep her calm and get back to some semblance of normality. "Sweetheart, settle down little bit, please," he said gently trying to calm her down.

"The vettig down below, said, we are having a son. And I was hoping that you would think that that was wonderful, just like me," she said. "Of course we won't know for sure, for another four weeks." Feeling he wasn't in tune with her desire.

"All right, all right, I just wanted you to settle down a little bit. We don't need you to stress out, you're pregnant," he said patronizingly.

"Okay, okay," she replied. Then she gave him a big kiss. After the little celebration they went to bed and fell asleep in each others arms.

The next day she woke up with her first bout of morning sickness. He chuckled to himself, as she headed to the facilities. Then he went over to the comm-panel and informed sick bay, that she would be taking the day off. The nurse that answered wondered whether or not, she needed anything. He just laughed and said no. Knowing that she was just fine. It was due to her condition, and he told the nurse just that. The nurse chuckled and said, I understand.

CHAPTER 7

As the Nova left orbit, a new chapter in the investigation was beginning. The vettigs had sent the information directly to the main computer as to how to find the elusive Luus. With that embedded in its core memory, they proceeded to the next set of coordinates. The captain had many questions, but the primary one was, what do we do with him when we find him? After all, he was a non-corporeal being how do you deal with that. Down in engineering, Tinker was trying to come up with a way to do just that. Then he had one of those epiphanies if he could not destroy such a being, then there may be a way to contain one. He then went about the task of designing such a weapon as that. He was going to be prepared, even if no one else would be.

The X0, was in the officer's mess eating with Lieut. May when the lieutenant asked, "do we really know what we're doing?"

"Son, this time, we are flying by the seat of our pants. We're making up everything as we go," replied the XO trying to make light of the situation.

"Well, I can tell you this, I'm a little frightened. And I'm not the only one," he informed the X0. "We're all a little on edge, not knowing what's going on."

"Son, this is where all that Imperial Fleet training comes in. Sometimes, you have to take things as they come," the XO said trying to put the lieutenant at ease.

"Well, as long as the captain knows what he's doing, I guess we'll be all right," he replied.

Just about that time, the captain came on the intercom trying to locate the X0. Having heard the hale, the XO went over to the comm-panel and flicked the switch and began to say, "the XO, here, sir."

"I need you on the bridge, right away," said the captain. Without hesitation, he headed to the bridge leaving his unfinished meal.

"What's going on?" He asked.

"We're at the first location that the vettig's put into the computer. Look for, your self," the captain said, indicating the screen with his eyes.

"Why that's the planet, Sarepta," an astonished XO said.

"Amazing, isn't it. The first place we encounter is in the heart of the Empire," the captain said.

It wasn't only the X0 that was amazed. When the chief engineer saw on his instruments where they were, even he in his wildest dreams didn't realize that there might be a possibility that the elusive Luus had an influence on his home world. Luus may have been the one to introduce discipline and the martial arts, to his planet. This influence may have been the very thing that saved his planet from annihilation could he be all bad he thought. His planet was heaped up in the middle of an immense civil war, with several factions fighting one another. He had read the historic accounts of a person coming on the scene and introducing discipline. He also, introduced an interesting concept that led the people of Sarepta to follow a different path, known as martial arts. Within the structure of the various types of martial arts, that was introduced to people they realized that they could control certain emotions. But, they saw the importance of certain emotions, those of a higher nobility, love, hope, and faith elements of the human expression that were not to be messed with. These were those concepts that were intrinsic to human survival and human nobility. His thoughts were this,'Luus', had some good in him. He didn't realize that a half truth was more dangerous than a lie. He had never encountered an evil such as this before.

The captain was formulating a plan of his own. He was hoping that diplomacy would win out. As they set up their orbit around the planet, he ordered, "get a hold of the Space Command and inform them that we need to come down and do a little research in their archives, Cmdr. Rahm." With that, the lieutenant commander did just that.

The Space Command issued the invitation to proceed. Then, the team that went to the planet was comprised of the science officer, the chief engineer, and the X0. The captain opted to stay on board ship, this time. He figured that he was not needed at this time. He felt that between the three he had chosen that he would get some answers. They used the smaller shuttle for their descent. When it landed, there was a welcoming committee from the Central Command, a branch of the Imperial Fleet. The Imperial Fleet has several bases strategically planted throughout the planet. The committee was comprised of a captain and one of his attachés. "Gentlemen, why are you here?" He asked.

"We need to get some information. I need to get into the archives," the science officer said.

"And I need to get a hold of one of my old teachers," said the chief engineer.

"And I'm here to inform your admiral about our progress. By now he knows what our mission is. And protocol calls for us to inform him and to have him relay that information," the XO said.

"Come this way, then," the captain said as he ushered them to his hovercraft. The hovercraft could hold several people at one time and was controlled by an on-board computer.

"Is this one of those new personnel carriers that has been issued to the military?" Asked the chief engineer, being inquisitive.

"No, it's not. This is one of the older models, all of the newer ones are on the planet, Sol.

They get all of the newer innovations, and we get their leftovers," the attaché said, with a little hesitation in his voice. He realized he was talking to a part of the crew from the flagship of the Imperial Fleet. He couldn't help himself from speaking, what was on his mind.

"Well, I've seen of few of the new ones back on, Sol. But I've never been inside one of them," the chief engineer replied.

"Then how do you get about the bases, there?" He asked.

"We have a car that we use," he replied.

"Is it your own? Or do they issue them to your crew?" He said, irreverently. Allowing his envy to be displayed.

"It's my own," he said nonchalantly. He wanted to downplay the attaché's envy.

When all was said and done, each one went to the separate locations they spoke of, respectively. The XO found himself going down another maze of corridors like back at the Military Citadel on Sol. This made him believe in the standardization of military infrastructures. All bases, must have similar buildings throughout the empire, he thought. As he arrived at the admiral's office, he noted that this admiral had a male version of a Ms. Roy. Even, right down to the headphones being on the right ear, and the microphone placed just off center, on his chest. He chuckled to himself and wondered if this was standard issue, too. "Is the admiral in?" The captain asked.

"Yes. He is," he said, irritatingly pointing to the door of the inner chamber. "He's expecting you. Go right on in." The secretary ordered.

"Commander," the admiral said as he saw him entering in. "Why do I have the pleasure of your company?"

"We needed to debrief, you, admiral, about everything that has happened so far," the XO replied. And with that, he began to tell, the admiral everything they had gone through up until then. Discretion was of a necessity in this being a complex issue. It was a matter of utmost the importance all involved. The admiral stamped the information top-secret-need-to-know.

The chief science officer went to the archives on the base having access to every archive on the planet that way. This made it easier to get access the information that they needed. The chief science officer enjoyed being in his element. He was learning, extemporaneously, about this mysterious stranger that averted the civil war of the planet.

The chief engineer was heading to the dojo of his old teacher, the one who taught him the form of martial arts he used. As he approached the compound, he watched the training exercises of several of the students, as his old teacher had expanded. He witnessed a match in the main court, as he was approaching, being careful not to disturb anything. He had slipped out of his shoes at the entrance to the court. He watched with the trained eye of a 10th class Drag-odo-kahn supreme master. This was the second highest rank in this martial art the highest being Ultra-supreme master. Only one other person on the planet had ever achieved such a distinction as an Ultra-supreme master and he was no longer living. That made the chief engineer, equal with approximately five others on the planet, including his old teacher. As the match ended, the chief engineer, applauded the match. Astonished everyone turned to see who it was, being rude, that was applauding. "That was a good match, but I saw a few flaws in their performance," he said smiling.

The champion of the match was irritated at the nonchalant manner of the visitor. He felt that he had given an excellent performance. "Would you care to elaborate," his old teacher, Rah Kahn said.

"I would be delighted," came his reply. With that he entered into the ring and bowed to his opponent.

His opponent returned the bow and said, "this will be a piece of cake." He smiled as he took the proper Drag-odo-kahn stance. Then he noted that his opponent stood in a modified stance such as the one he saw the teacher use from time to time. The thought went through his head, who is this? The match began and was over in seconds with the chief engineer, still standing, and his opponent was on the ground unconscious.

"You haven't lost a step. Have you?" The master asked. "Students this is Jef Bel." Then everyone understood knowing the name very well.

"No I haven't. And I have a gained a few more over the years to add to my repertoire. But, that is not why I'm here," he said. He wasn't the type to put on airs he had done what he needed.

"That was obvious. People! The tournament is over for the time being," he announced. As he got up from his seat to usher the chief engineer, through a passageway that was behind his chair. The others that were left behind helped the unconscious student to his feet as he gained consciousness. The passage led to an underground entrance to the living quarters of the master. Only those having reached the eighth level of the red belt, knew of its existence, the red belt being the highest belt of this order. "Would you like some nourishment, or something?" He being the good host asked, as he was pointing to some food that was on a table, a humble setting of rice and herbs, as they arrived at their final destination.

"No, thank you. But I'll have some tea. Then I'll proceed with why I'm here," he replied. With that the master poured both of them a cup of tea. "I'm on an investigation, and you may have some information that I need," he continued.

"What might that be?" He asked.

"Well, you remember the old stories of the beginning of our peace. You know what I'm talking about, the mysterious stranger that arrived with the answer, just before we tried to annihilate ourselves?" he said.

"Continue," he said, as there was a pause in the chief engineers questioning.

"I need to know if you remember what his name was?" He asked.

"I believe it was Lucius, meaning enlightened one. Everyone was amazed that his name was actually a title given to 'the messengers' written in the Holy Chronicles. At least, that's the way I remember it," came his reply.

"I thought that's the way it was," the chief engineer said.

"Will you be leaving right away? I've missed your friendship," Master Kahn said with a heavy heart reflecting in his face, anticipating his reply.

"Yes, I have to. But you have helped me quite a bit. You don't know what this means to all of us. But I'll come back soon. I miss your company, too," he replied. And with that, he left to meet up with the others.

"Yes, I believe I do know what it means," the master said looking up as he watched his friend leave.

As the other two approached the landing dock where the shuttle was, the chief engineer met them, along the way. The science officer's eyes and the chief engineer's eyes met. Both knew instinctively that the other one had some information vital to this mission. The XO was oblivious to this and lead the way to the shuttle. Once inside, it was relatively quiet as they journeyed back to the ship allowing for everyone to reflect on everything that they learned. Once on board, the XO announced over the intercom, their arrival. With that the captain called for another senior staff meeting, including the security officer once more.

As everyone was gathered around the table, a new chair had been added to the seating arrangement, it was the one for the security officer, Jonz. "Gentlemen, what did you learn? The captain asked.

"Well, captain, I learned from the archives that there was a mysterious stranger named Lucius. He talked with the heads of the seven factions back in the day. I mean, when there was a civil war being fought on Sarepta. He helped them recognize that they needed discipline, and that they could do it themselves. He further explained to them that love, hope, and they were ideologies to be left alone. I guess he didn't want to alarm any of the other vettigs by going too far," he explained.

"Anything, else, gentlemen?" the captain inquired.

"I learned from my old teacher that Lucius, meant enlightened one," the chief engineer added. "And that he was thought of as some sort of Messiah, to my people."

"Well, that remains to be seen. We need to begin to go to the next level of the investigation. XO, what does the computer say, we have to do next?" The captain asked.

"It says that we have to go on another journey," he said as he looked at the message with astonishment. This was not the normal response from the computer. It seemed a more of a human response. But he kept that to himself, making everyone think that he was paraphrasing the computer.

Then they proceeded to do just that as the computer said. Laying in their course from there and returning to their duty stations. "How's the doctor?" The captain inquired in the lift speaking to the chief science officer, taking note of her obvious absence.

"She's doing fine. She's being normal for her condition, this morning," came the reply.

"I'm just being concerned," the captain said.

The science officer was rather relieved that somebody else besides himself was concerned about his wife. The emotions that he exhibited were not the norm for him. The captain noticed this and began to think about what he was getting himself into, with his impending nuptials. But he put it out of his mind, the mission was more important at this time if they failed there might not be an Empire to have a wedding in. The Nova went on its way on the course that the computer had laid in. It felt as if they were flying blind. Where was this taking them to next? Was the purveying thought of the entire senior staff. But they would know soon enough in their estimation. There was no need to second-guess what was going to be. It was about this time, that the doctor had a vision in her living quarters between the bouts of vomiting from her morning sickness. She envisioned a great battle being waged in the cosmos. Two great warriors with swords and shields, wearing armor indicative of early Sol, appeared before her. She saw both had helmets with feathers sticking out of the Mohawk-style of metal that protruded out of its crown with a leather chin strap. And she also saw the breastplates of metal that they wore with different insignias engraved on each, they were held on with leather straps that buckled in the back. Then she saw their pelvic the regions covered with what looked like formfitting metal girdles. Then she noticed metal shin guards that were strapped on with leather as well. They were connected to metal feet covers by metal rings forming a hinge for flexibility. As she saw the battle ensuing, she noticed that both had great skills in their techniques, having been a fencer herself in college. It looked like they were in a dead heat, one not winning over the other. Then the vision stopped. She couldn't understand what was going on. Was she hallucinating do to the overwhelming increase of hormones in her system do to her condition or was it something else. She did not want to alarm her husband so she kept this to herself. As far as she was concerned, there was no need to worry anyone. But she pondered in her heart meaning anyway. After all, it could be a real vision that was being given her. But by who? She shrugged.

Meanwhile, back on the Star Blaster, the colonel was observing every move that the Nova was making. He had many questions, but no answers. His crew followed him without doubt. He had put the fear of a thousand deaths in their head. He realized, in his estimation, that intimidation was the best key to a command. This was a way of life for all those that were in charge of something, from the Prime Minister on down, intimidation. The XO, the science officer, was extrapolating the data necessary trying to give meaning to everything that was going on. He wanted to be on top of things, just in case. He was waiting for his opportunity to take over as commander of the ship. That is why he made meticulous entries into a special log that he kept. He wanted everything to be verified. This was a common practice among subordinates throughout the Cabal Union, an unwritten rule. This was the way the Union did its checks and balances. With the right information, you could go clear to the top. It was hard for them to carry out their mission statement, conquer, enslave, corrupt, use, and abuse with the Empire in the mix. Even though, this statement was not written down anywhere, it was an implication from their practices in the past. It had been a while since the Union added any worlds to their roster. On the other hand, the empire had annexed several. With several worlds as friends. Those that were contemplating joining or those that did not join the Union, over the years, were considered friends. The colonel was hoping that whatever it was that they were investigating would help the Union get the upper hand on the Empire. A much-needed in fusion of new worlds would give the Union a better circumstance in all of its affairs. Even though they were a superpower in the galaxy, they knew that the Empire really had the upper hand. Because of that, the Titanium Barrier, the border between the two superpowers as it's called, had not been breached by either side, until now for quite some time. But, soon, the Nova would be heading into Union Space. And the colonel was taking note of that when, they fell into some turbulence themselves. "What was that?" The colonel asked.

"That was turbulence, sir," came the reply from the helmsman. "I am compensating for it with our inertial dampeners." Then he pressed a couple of buttons on his console.

"Sir, the turbulence was caused by a familiar anomaly. It was a quantum stream," the XO explained.

"A quantum stream out here?" The colonel asked astonished.

"Quantum streams can pop up anywhere, and once they have. They stabilize in that area after a period of time," explained the XO. " Furthermore, they must be explored to find out where they go."

"I understand the science of it all. I was just surprised that we would run into one, here," the colonel explained.

Quantum streams were discovered a millennia ago and made it possible to traverse great distances in a matter of seconds instead of light-years. This allowed for both of the super powers to build themselves up. It also gave meaning to the phrase, it's a small universe, commonly used in conversations on both sides. This is how they made many of their discoveries. It also allowed, sometimes, for them to bypass each other's territories. This aided in the peace process between the two.

"Have you recorded the coordinates?" The colonel asked.

"We've noted it in the ship's log, sir," replied the XO. The notation read just inside the Titanium Barrier on the Union's side was a quantum stream, with coordinates applicable. The Star Blaster was following the Nova into their own space. They kept themselves remarkably, invisible. They could have confronted the other ship, but they wanted to see where it would lead them. It wouldn't take long for them to find out, as the Nova arrived at its destination. It was a small, alpha-classed planet as they had encountered in the unknown portion where they had gotten the message from Luus. As the Nova scanned the planet, but no people just as the other mysterious planet revealed. This meant that they could use the translation device, as they had before. There were no dampening fields, around this planet, because there were no people to man, any such devices. There weren't any devices at all that they knew of. This time, the team was headed by the chief security officer, Neh Miah, the son of the Chief Science Director, that was instrumental in starting this whole thing, the security officer, Jonz, the one that accompanied the landing party the first time where this all began, a med tech, and one of the other subordinate science officers. The captain wanted to keep the senior staff out of harms way by wisely choosing this team. They could gather the information that they needed just as well as anybody else. He had a good crew under him. Planet side the team began scanning the area. They extrapolated all of the information from their scans and begin fanning out to further the scan of the planet. The security officer, Jonz, recognize a cave that looked like the twin to the other one where this part of the investigation began, at least for him. "Lieutenant Commander, over here!" He yelled. The lieutenant commander came running to where he was, along with the others. They all gathered together at the entrance of the cave. The security officer was looking for a triggering device. The others stood around dumbfounded at what he was doing, but they did not say a word for fear of being thought they were ignorant.

"There it is. That's what I'm looking for," he said with relief.

"What is it that you are looking for?" Asked the chief security officer.

"The triggering device," he said. "There is no need for an alarm. It it will only trigger another message, when we get inside." He showed how knowledgeable he was exhibiting pride. Then he led the rest of the team inside as though he was in charge. Inside, he found out he was right. It was another holographic image just like before. But there was a difference here, the image was that of a different person. It still appeared to be man-like just as before but with different features. The others marveled at the sight, but the security officer held his peace. His knowledge of such things was being evidenced. "My name is Biel and I have been banished to this world. If you are hearing this message. I have escaped. And will try to find my comrade in arms, Luus. We are vettigs, a non-corporeal being made up of pure energy. This image you see is utilized to interact with mankind..." With that, the security officer found the source of the message in a similar place to the first message he had witnessed. He proceeded to do what he had done before, and shut it off to extrapolate the message, placing it on his scanner. Then they left the cave and the chief security officer pressed the buttons on his communicator, that was situated around his neck, and then gave the order for them to be translated up.

Then, the captain met them. He wanted to debrief them, himself. As the chief security officer gave his report, the security officer Jonz gave him his scanner. "Thank you. Your discretion is necessary, top secret, that's an order," the captain said. Everyone in the debriefing, understood. Then the captain found himself wondering, what was he going to do with two of them, if, they were together. He needed to get some perspective on this and asked for his closest confidante's to meet him in the doctor's living quarters. The science officer and the doctor were all ready there. The chief engineer and the XO rendezvoused with the captain at the same time. The captain was holding the scanner with the new message. He wanted this meeting to be hush-hush, this was to be a very top-secret meeting. With this news he wanted the crew to be ignorant for their own sake. It would be hard enough for the few that already knew to understand it. He knew what the ramifications could be. And he knew the questions that would arise from the information. "Friends, I really need your counsel. We have another matter that has come up," he said being a bit cryptic. With that, he plugged the scanner into the view-screen. Then, he began the new message. They watched the entire message to completion. There was a dead silence, it was a type of silence that would wake the dead, that screamed so loud. "As you can see. I really need your help," the captain, breaking the silence admitted.

They all took a moment to gather their thoughts. It was the good doctor that began the conversation. "I think that it would be, behoove us to begin with prayer to guide our actions," she said with great concern. The others nodded their heads in agreement, and then bowed their heads, to do just that.

"Please, Grand Designer, help us in our time of need. We need guidance and a little courage in this hour of desperation.

We have learned a new chapter in our history. All we need is a little help to understand it all," the science officer respect fully requested. It was his wife, the doctor, that was surprised at who was praying. Everyone felt relieved and collectively said, amen. As they paused to think over what they were going to say, the bells and whistles for the general quarters sounded. "What now," the XO said disappointingly. "Interruptions, now!" Then everybody headed for their duty stations, including the doctor this time.

As the XO, chief science officer, and the captain arrived on the bridge. The blast doors were down, and the view-screen was on. The helmsman, the one that had the command-duty was the one that sounded general quarters. "What's going on, lieutenant?" The captain asked as he took his chair. The XO remained standing.

"There is a ship of unknown origin, approaching us on an intercept course. We we haven't seen this type of configuration before, except when we were back at Eden," the lieutenant replied.

As the captain saw the scene. He wondered if his friends from Eden had come to lend them a hand. "Hale them!" The captain commanded.

"Giving the hale. Receiving transmission, and there is video," Lieut. Cmdr. Rahm replied.

"On screen!" Came the command.

"Hello! My name is Biel. Why are you here? You are violating my space," a familiar figure to the three senior officers. There was quite a pause before anybody replied to what seemed like a threatening message. The captain wanted to pick his words, precisely so as not to arouse this being's suspicions. He didn't need a confrontation at this time.

CHAPTER 8

After he had taken the time to gather his thoughts he began his ploy. "I didn't realize that there was anybody rich enough to own their own planet. We are sorry for the whole situation," the captain replied. "We'll leave the same way we came in peace."

"That's quite all right. I enjoy having visitors. If you would care to meet me down on the surface. We could have a respite, together," he said being very polite.

"It will take us a few moments to gather ourselves together. Should we say, one hour?" The captain said.

"That will be fine with me. It will give me some time to make arrangements for suitable delicacies to be served at such an auspicious occasion as this," the mysterious figure, said.

With that the XO sliced his hand across his neck to tell the comm-officer to end transmissions. "Then, let's give him a visit," the XO said, with more curiosity than fear in his voice.

"You, me, and security officer Jonz," he ordered, nodding his head.

"Captain, shouldn't I go with you?" The science officer asked.

"No arguments. My orders stand," came the reply from the captain. With that the XO and the captain went to the translation room and were met there by the security officer, having gotten the orders via the intercom. With that, the three stepped up on the pads and the captain gave the order as he had so many times before, "begin translation."

The scene on the surface had a different landscape than before. The security officer was surprised to see an edifice where there was not one before, having landed at the exact coordinates, that they landed at the first time he was there. With an inquisitive look he followed the others into the edifice. Inside the mysterious stranger was already seated at a table set for a king. There were all sorts of sumptuous goodies that men delighted themselves in. "Welcome! I hope this meets with your approval. I would like to take some time to explain," Biel said.

The captain and his companions sat themselves down, but stayed alert. "We have a few questions of our own. May we ask them?" He said being polite.

"Why are you being so diplomatic. Ask away!" He said with a big smile on his face. In his mind. He was about ready to upset the plans of the Grand Designer.

"Let me start with, who are you? Or rather, what are you?" The captain asked.

"You were here before? And you have my message? Why do I need to explain anything?" Beil inquired with a smile.

"Yes, we have. But we would like to hear from the horse's mouth. We are curious about everything," the security officer said in anticipation of the others thoughts.

"Well, let me see where to begin. I am Beil. I come from another dimension that we call the Paradise of Light. We have been sent here to bring enlightenment to mankind. My name in my native tongue means believer. Is that what you wanted, captain?" Came his explanation.

"That'll do for a start. What I would like to know is, if you found your comrade in arms, Luus?" The captain asked.

"Why, yes, I have," came his reply, smiling.

"And where is he now?" The XO asked.

"He's on a mission right now," came the reply, being rather cryptic.

Luus was on a mission. He was trying to recruit others to his cause. The mysterious signature that they detected was exactly like the other vettig ships that they registered at Eden. Therefore, this made it hard to tell the good guys from the bad. But the aforementioned mission was not finished. Only the two, Luus and Beil knew what that mission was all about.

"What kind of mission, would that be?" Asked the XO continuing the engagement with the vettig.

"That is a matter between he and I . Besides, we haven't finished our respite," trying to misdirect the situation.

"It looks like a good meal," the captain interrupted.

"It is! You'll love the Empress fish caviar, it's the finest in all the galaxy. And I recommend that you try the royal bird it is scrumptious, roasted to perfection," he said with a hint of gleefulness in his voice. With that, they began to eat. The captain kept in mind his own precautions that he had given to everyone else.

Back on the ship, the science officer was scanning the other ship for any other anomalies. He wondered if a ship of that size, had a crew. But their scanners could not penetrate it. The chief engineer, had the command. The doctor was in sick bay, doing an inventory of supplies, just in case there was any trouble. It was the helmsman's alertness that alerted everybody to the new ship in the area. The ship scans had detected the Star Blaster. The Star Blaster had let her guard down. But they were not aware that the Nova knew that. The chief engineer, ordered that there was to be a red alert. Having noticed that the Star Blaster was hovering not moving in any direction. He amended his order to a modified yellow alert, he figured that they were just trying to ascertain whether or not, the Nova had hostile intentions. Besides, they were only a few clicks inside the Titanium Barrier there was no need for hostilities on either side. Maybe they thought they were on a survey mission, not realizing they had reached the Titanium Barrier, he would give them the benefit of the doubt. He knew the Union had a standing order, act, then ask questions. This he knew because of the prior dealings he had had personally with them.

"She could do anything, Sir," the navigator said. He showed his concern about their predicament.

"No. Just keep alert. We'll deal with them, when we have to," the chief engineer replied.

While this was all going on, the chief science officer was doing a little investigation of his own. He was not concerned with what was going on out there, rather, he was concerned about what was going on on the surface. His investigation was a correlation of the two messages. He was a good scientist that made backups to backups, and he wanted to compare both messages using the backup that he had of the first with the other message he had. His conclusions were that the two vettigs were indeed comrades, but there was a little bit of envy between the two. This revelation might come in handy later on down the road. He made a notation of this. It seemed like someone or something was guiding his hand. He also noted that Beil was a little more forthcoming with his explanation of things. This made him wonder if the two vettigs were equals, or not. It was his understanding that a small minority of vettigs had gone over to their side and were banished similar to what they had been. According to his message about one fourth of the vettigs from the Paradise of Light had gone with them. What had they gotten themselves into the science officer thought. Would they have to go to all of the planets where these beings were banished to? This and many other questions crossed, the chief science officer's mind. Maybe, he could find a way to destroy beings such as this by carefully studying the two messages and the archives on board ship. He rerouted everything from his duty station to his work station in his living quarters. Then he turned his attentions to the scanners, leaving everything else on the back burner.

Back on the surface, the captain and his entourage were still interrogating their mysterious host. They had learned a little more about the struggle between the vettigs in the grand designer. From that they ascertained that it was a one-sided skirmish. From their observation Beil was not telling the whole truth. Then, the captain formulated a way to return to the ship. He was trying to appear to be a grateful guest. back to his ship. There was no need to cause any alarm to his host. With that in mind, he said, "we need to be getting back to the ship. We are very grateful for your generosity and your hospitality. But there are some procedures that we need to go over before we can spread your message."

"But, captain, there's no need to be in a rush. But if there is a need, there is a need," he said bowing to protocol.

"We also need to check with our ship to see if there has been anything new. With your permission," he said.

"By all means, if you need to, do so," he gave them permission.

With the permission given they left the edifice to be translated up as a part of their checks as they had explained. Back on the ship captain began to ask, "what's our status?"

"There's then a new wrinkle in our situation, captain, a new ship has been spotted," the translation engineer said.

"Is it one of their's?" He asked.

"No, sir. It's one of the Union ships, sir," came the reply.

With that the three men entered the corridor to head down to the lift. As the captain gave the command to go to the bridge he turned to the security officer that was with them and said, "you're with me." The security officer nodded his head. It seemed like he was really in the thick of things. "Gentlemen, what is our status?" The captain said, taking his seat. He stationed the security officer at the rail behind him.

"It's just sitting out there. Doing nothing. What are your orders?" The XO said, moving over to his chair because the captain had taken over.

"Just keep alert. I see that you have done the right thing. There will be a debriefing of all senior staff in half an hour. We need to see where we stand at this moment. That will be all, gentlemen," he ordered announcing it over the intercom to those that weren't in close proximity of his voice.

Again, they met in the conference room, everyone taking their seat. The captain opened the meeting and began to rehearse everything that happened to them on the surface. As everyone thought for a few moments it was the science officer that broke the silence. "I have transferred all of the data to my workstation in my living quarters concerning this situation. If I could be given the opportunity to study it. I may be able to find a way out of this whole mess. Or at least be able to cope with what lies ahead," he said.

"That will be satisfactory. By all means go to your living quarters and do just that. Doctor, I need your aid in a little something as well. I need you to go over any of the scanning logs to see if there is some way we can exploit any weaknesses in our host. And Tinker, I know you have been in the planning stages of a weapon. But, we need more than theories. We need a real weapon," the captain said.

"I have something on paper, captain, I need to put together a prototype. It will take a little time," he replied.

"How much time do you need?" He asked.

"It'll take a little time, about, an hour," he replied.

"You have 45 minutes. No more, no less," he ordered. Tinker just shrugged in agreement.

"Is there anything you want me to do, captain?" the security officer asked.

"I need you, Jonz, to get with your department head and fill him in on everything. I need him to be up to speed. Having someone tell him firsthand what's going on will help him and us," the captain said. Even though, the security officer was right there. He wanted to give credence to the chain of command. This brought the security officer back to his room position in all of this. He realized he was crucial just for the moment. Making this an awkward moment for him. He'd gotten used to being around the inner circle of the ship.

Down on the surface, the vettig was sending out a message of his own into a part of space unknown. His communications was to his comrade, Luus. It wasn't that he needed back up but he thought that it would be a good idea to have him along. The frequency that he used was undetected by either ship in orbit.

It was rather interesting to him to realize how limited, these beings were. He wondered why the Grand Designer had an interest in beings such as these. After all, they weren't like he was, a non-corporeal being. The Holy Chronicles explained that these beings were created beings, having limitations nothing like he was. The messengers of light, as they were called it in the Holy Chronicles were beings that were created to be of a help to mankind, rather than a hindrance he had placed this aside. During 'the great struggle' those that were left behind did the same without question. And those that were banished were left to their own devices. In the very moment of banishment, any free will, that they had was eliminated because their choice had been made, where mankind had not made that choice yet. Free will was still in play, according to the Holy Scriptures, at this time. This was explained in no uncertain terms in both the Old Tribute and the New Tribute portions of the Holy Chronicle.

"Captain, I need you to come to my quarters," the science officer said over the intercom.

The captain understood. And made his way to the science officers quarters, hoping that he had something new to report. As he stood outside the hatch of the science officers living quarters, he thought to himself, maybe we'll get some answers now. He pushed the button which made a chime on the other side of the hatch. "Enter!" The science officer ordered. With that the hatch slid open. And the captain entered in.

"Hal, do you have anything?" Came the inquiry from the captain as he entered in.

"Yes, sir, I think I have. As I was studying the data I realized two things: 1. The two vettigs in question had a rivalry. 2. If we pit one against the other, we may have a chance. Also, the

Grand Designer has the ability to destroy these beings if he so desired," the science officer reported.

"That doesn't help much. We have no way of getting a hold of the Grand Designer to get him to help us. Or even to know if he had the desire. But maybe we have a chance with the other," he said thoughtfully.

"That was what I was thinking," said the science officer.

"Not to change the subject, but is your wife up to the task at hand?" Asked the captain.

"Yes, sir, she is. We have both been talking, and it looks like she is able to cope with her morning sickness. She has come up with a new therapy that does not interfere with the natural order of things. She's back to work now," he replied.

"That's excellent. I need all of my 'brain trust' at their best. Right now, we need to figure out what we're going to do with the situation at hand," the captain said.

With that, he turned and went to engineering for the next part of his odyssey. He was on a mission to make sure everyone was secure in their duties of the moment. The science officer continued his research to make sure he didn't miss anything. As the captain arrived at an engineering, he emerged to see the chief engineer testing his new weapon. It was some sort of molecular scrambler. He pointed it at a large beam of metal he placed upright in the middle of the room. He was behind a screen to protect himself as the atoms scattered throughout the room. The captain shielded himself by covering his face with his arms. "Quite impressive," the captain said.

"Thank you, captain," the chief engineer replied. "I need to tweak it a little bit. It's just a prototype. I need to see if it will work on energy. You know what I mean?" He asked not realizing he had just missed the captain's face with all the debris.

"No. I don't. I'm not as adept in matters like this, as you are," he replied.

"If we can disperse energy with this weapon, then we will have something that we can use against the vettigs," he said.

"I'm beginning to understand now. You're not changing energy, but dispersing it," the captain said.

"That's right, captain, that's exactly right," he replied.

Neither one of them understood that the energy that had coalesced into making these beings, was attached to an intelligentsia. And they did not take into account the possibility that this intelligentsia may make these beings invulnerable to any such weapon. They just thought that it would work. And they never took into account their design. That design was what made them what they were.

"Good thinking, Tinker," the captain said with appreciation. With that he left engineering and went to sick bay. As he entered sick bay, he saw the doctor at her desk, which was her work station. She viewing her research.

"Captain, there may be a way that we could use vibrations against the vettigs," she informed him.

"Anything we can come up with, doctor, would be of a help. Compare notes with the chief engineer. I believe he is on a similar track," the captain informed her. "I'll be heading back to the bridge."

"I' ll do just that," she replied.

The captain, finished his odyssey with the bridge as his final destination. With everything that he had learned he needed to get with the XO in regards to what they were going to do next. As the plan was being formulated by the two they wanted it only to be between them. There was no need to get anybody else involved, in case it didn't work. The chief engineer was a good commander and the science officer would make a good

XO. If, they did not succeed. And the captain knew that. So he wanted to limit any fallout just in case.

On the Star Blaster, they noticed the ship that was orbiting the planet with the Nova had the same signature as what they saw before, but now a secondary signature was being indicated by their scanners. A new vessel was arriving. It, also, had the exact same signature. If they were not seeing it with their own eyes, they would've thought it was this same exact ship. This made the colonel suspicious. What was going on over there? Maybe he should move in. "Move in! Set up an orbit on the opposite side of the planet. We need to see what's going on," the colonel ordered.

As the Star Blaster entered into their orbit, the Nova sounded general quarters. The flashing lights and the bells and whistles went off. "What are they doing?" The captain inquired.

"I believe that they are heading to the other side of the planet. I'm not quite for sure," the navigator said as he was watching them on the screen make their maneuvers. He also checked his control panel that gave telemetry for the other ship.

As the other ship went out of their site, the captain ordered the stand down from general quarters. He realized what they were doing. If it was the other way around, he would've done the same thing. After all, they were in their neck of the woods. Maybe, this could be the break that they were needing. Realizing that there was another shortcoming, he needed an element of surprise and maybe the Star Blaster had provided that. Maybe the plan that he formulated would work. The hairs on his head were still standing, indicating that there was still a bit of danger ahead. But, he didn't allow anyone else to know.

As the Star Blaster set up its orbit they translated themselves to the surface, immediately. Their landing party was comprised of the colonel, two security officers, and one of the lower science officers. The colonel wanted someone along to help explain things if need be. The two security officers were normal for this type of operation. They had translated themselves to a set of coordinates about one quarter click from the edifice. As they got nearer, the structure the security officers set up a multi-functional, multi-directional metabolic mike. Standard issue to all landing parties of the Union's fleet. This was set up so that they could record any and all conversations for security purposes. Then the data collected by the microphone would then be relayed back to the ship. Then the colonel proceeded with his entourage to the edifice. It was an amazing sight, because they knew that this planet was supposed to be uninhabited. The last time any ships had been this way it was reported that there were no structures, let alone any inhabitants on this planet. The colonel had checked the data archives of his ship for any such information as this. So, he wasn't sure what he would find.

"Gentlemen! Welcome!" The mysterious stranger said with a half baked smile on his face as the entourage approached.

"Hello. How do you do? What are you doing here?" The colonel inquired indignantly.

"Why, what do you mean, colonel?" The stranger inquired.

"Who are you? What is your purpose here? Why are you in Cabal Union space?" He inquired again with a little indignation in his tone.

"Colonel, if you'll check your records. You will see that I am the owner of this planet. I'll present you with the paperwork. Come this way," Beil said. With that and they went inside the edifice with him leading the way.

"You say you have some paperwork? When did you receive it? The Cabal Union very seldom gives anything like that to an individual," he said perplexed.

"They did me. Prime Minister Bil Kahn was the one that issued them to me," came his reply.

"That was five prime ministers ago. You must have an inherited this place," he said.

"No, it was me. Prime Minister Kahn issued these papers to me himself. I'm older than I look," he said laughing at their perplexed looks.

"You still haven't answered who you are. Nor have you given me your purpose," he said.

"We can talk about that in a moment. Right now, I'm being remiss in my duties as host, some refreshments," he said as he extended his arm toward the table that seemed to appear out of nowhere, having not noticed it before.

"Colonel, we are bit hungry," one of the security guards said being out of character. Security guards of the Cabal Union were usually quiet and never said anything.

"Be seated." The colonel ordered feeling a little hungry himself. Their insubordination, never registered with him.

"I take it that you are not with the other ship, are you? And then they have not shared with you any information," Beil said.

"How can I put this diplomatically, we're not really friends," the colonel informed him.

"I understand. Maybe, I can be of help to you," he smiled, realizing that they were of the Cabal Union.

"What do you mean by that?" He asked.

"Well, I have power that you know not of. In fact, I believe, a friend of mine has arrived. As we speak," he said. With that, he stood up and went out. As everyone inside the edifice was eating the colonel got up to tag along being a few steps behind. To his amazement when he caught up he saw two beings, almost translucent, touching one another. He wondered what kind of beings these were. He had never before in all of his service to the Union seen anything quite like this. His curiosity overrode his fear. Then the two beings were solid, and the mass and form and doing so right in front of him. He just shook his head and proceeded inside quickly so as not to arouse suspicion figuring they had not seen him.

"Gentlemen, this is my good friend and comrade, Luus," he said as he entered the edifice once more with his comrade in tow.

"Please to meet you, gentlemen," he said with a smile on his face. "I understand that there may be something we could help you with. Beil explained to me a little bit about your situation."

"Maybe, we can be of a mutual assistance to one another," the colonel said.

Back on the Nova the captain and his entourage of confidants were getting together in the science officer's living quart's. The captain was looking over everything that was laid out on the table in front of him. They were giving him recommendations, and he was taking it all in. He believed that they now had a plan that he was confident in. Now they could proceed, all systems go. But, he felt that there was something missing. He could not put his finger on it. "People, we have a plan," he announced. They were all pleased with themselves. But, in the back of their minds they hoped that they could accomplish what they set out to do. What the others didn't know was that the X0, and the captain had a plan B., just in case.

On the surface the colonel and his entourage were planning some things of their own. The two vettigs had convinced them that they were on their side. Luus had scanned the Star Blaster's computer archives to get a little bit more information on the Union's history to add to the transfer of information he had gotten from Beil when they were in their translucent state. This was done without the knowledge of anyone of the Star Blaster. It was a very interesting read. He had learned that the Union had been influenced by his comrade, Beil. It was Beil that had convinced the home world of the Union, Rama, to begin conquering their part space through intimidation. He then set up a series of secret societies. He ascertained that the information he received from Beil was truthful. It was quite the experiment. He was pleased with the results. This was the type of work he knew would be helpful. He was glad that his comrade had been working so hard toward their mutual goals. His stay back on the planet of his banishment had taught him to be patient. But his patience was growing thin. It was his time to try to do as much mischief as he possibly could. After all, he was going to replace the Grand Designer. At least that's what he thought.

The captain had chosen a new landing party comprised of himself, the chief security officer, the chief engineer, and his chief science officer. The chief security officer was equipped with a second weapon similar to the one that the chief engineer had assembled. The chief engineer kept the original prototype. They had translated themselves down to the planet's surface a bit further away from the edifice this time. The next step was to proceed with caution. As they came near the object of their destination, they were surprised by the colonel. The colonel had captured the whole landing party. "My dear, captain, we meet for the first time," he said, gritting his teeth together.

"My pleasure," the captain said sarcastically.

"Captain, I am pleased to meet you, also," Luus said. The captain recognized him right away from message number one. His likeness was emblazoned in his memory, as was Beil's.

"Luus, I presume," he said.

"So, you've heard of me?" He asked with pride.

"Sort of," came the reply. "I saw your message back on another planet. You know, the one where you were trapped." He was taunting him.

"Ahh! I understand. You're trying some sort of tactic on me," he said perceptively.

"Is it working?" He said quizzically. At least he still had his sense of humor at this time, marveled.

"I've had better then you try things like that," he said getting serious. "Captain, I'm a reasonable person."

"Person? I don't think so. Because a real person would use diplomacy rather than violence," he stated. Looking around at all of the hardware being pointed at him.

"I'm all for diplomacy, as long as I'm holding the gun," he replied laughing from a vantage point of strength.

"So, that's why Beil, here's been building up your empire," he was putting your plan into place.

"What do you mean by his empire?" Beil said, with indignation. "His plan."

Then the colonel realized what was going on. And he decided to switch loyalties realizing that being such as this could not be trusted. "Yes, it stands to reason it's his empire. After all, he looks like he's the stronger of the two of you," he said chiming in with the captain. He realized that the Union he loved so much was being threatened.

"Besides, Luus, you would be the better monarch. You know what I mean?" The captain asked. He fed right into his ego. With that, the two vettigs began arguing with each other. The captain motioned for him and the colonel along with the others to clear out of there.

"Colonel, we must get back to our ships," the captain whispered.

"Captain, I already have you in my custody, but I agree we must get out of here. If, I let you go to your ship. What's in it for me?" The colonel asked.

"We'll send you all of the data concerning our most recent investigation, the thing you've stumbled on here," the captain said, pointing to the ground.

"I have a different idea. Your men can go to their ship. You stay with me until I get the data you so amply want to supply," the colonel said.

"That'll be just fine. Let's just get out of here. So we can regroup," the captain agreed thinking of his men.

With that they headed to the ships as they had planned. On board, the captain saw for the first time, what a Cabal Union ship looked like being a guest. He was rather impressed at their technology. But, it was not much different than that of the Empire's. But, he still didn't feel safe. Not because he was on a Union ship, but because of they were still orbiting around the planet. And down below were two beings of immense power. They needed to put as much distance between them and themselves. "May I contact my ship to let them know I'm okay and to have them transmit the data we talked about?" The captain asked.

"By all means do so," replied the colonel. With that the captain pressed his communicator's send buttons and began transmitting the order. The colonel knew that the captain couldn't do anything sneaky. They have their shields up, which prohibited the usage of a translator.

"Bar, XO, are we receiving a stream of data from the Nova?" The colonel asked from the communication panel on their translation computer, having been translated up. He didn't want to allow the captain to have the free reign of his ship. He wanted to limit his movements for security sake. After all, he didn't want any of the ship's secrets going over to the other side.

"We're receiving it now," came the reply.

"Captain, it has been a pleasure," he said. "You're free to go. Sergeant, send him over to the other ship," he ordered.

With that the captain was translated over to his ship. He then began ordering his ship to be underway. He wanted to put as much distance between that planet and his ship as he could. And they began to do just that. They retraced the course that the Star Blaster used to get into Union space. It was stellar topography that contacted the bridge to tell the captain who had just arrived that they had just discovered the same anomaly, as did the Star Blaster, the quantum stream. That gave the captain an idea. "Has it stabilized?" He asked.

"Yes, it has, sir," came the reply.

"Helm, head right for the quantum stream. We don't have time, to explore it to see where it

goes. We just have to go," he ordered. Because the dynamics of a quantum stream were very complex. Scans were useless at this time, they just had to go by the seat of their pants.

"Aye! Aye! Captain," replied the helmsman. With that, they headed towards the quantum stream. The captain knew that quantum streams covered great distances in space. He just didn't know which direction this one went. Do to the exploration of others, and the mapping thereof, they knew where these other streams went. New ones had to be explored for all sorts of safety purposes. But they didn't have time for this right now. The safety of the ship was the preeminent thought.

Upon entering the quantum stream, they began scanning it. As the data was being correlated and routed to the science officer's duty station on the bridge the science officer noticed how remarkably stable it was. This made him come to the conclusion that this anomaly have been there for quite some time, not knowing that it had just been created. Scans had no way of telling how old quantum streams really were. This was do to all of the interference from the quantum fluctuations in its barriers. When dealing with time, it was tricky. The science officer knew all of the theories behind quantum streams but they were just that, theories.

"Captain, we are receiving telemetry on the anomaly, right now. Transferring conclusions to your panel," the science officer said.

As the captain studied the screen, that was a attached to the arm of his chair, he noted that, they were going a shorter distance than the usual quantum stream afforded. But, he still wasn't for sure which direction. But he felt a little safer putting as much distance between him and his adversaries. Then they reached the end of the quantum stream in a matter of seconds. They came out within a two-hour journey to the planet, Eden. He then ordered the communication officer to hale the planet and let them know that they needed to set up an orbit again. They returned the hale and agreed.

"Captain, the planet, Eden has given specific orders as how to proceed. They said that they wanted you and the doctor and the chief science officer to be the landing party this time," comm-officer said.

"That'll be just fine. I'll issue the orders right away. Hal, you're with me. XO, Pappy, you're in charge. We're going down there. And make sure that the doctor knows to meet us in the translation room," the captain said.

The good doctor had made it to the translation room seconds before the captain and her husband, the science officer. She was ready for anything, right about now. The captain exhibited relief knowing that there were twice as many good vettigs on their side at this time. With that he ordered the translation to begin. "There's been a new development," the captain said addressing Enosh, the first person he saw when they were retranslated into their normal state.

"What is it?" He asked.

"Not only have we found Luus we have found Beil as well. How many of these beings are there?" He asked.

"There's quite a few of us. But, you need not concern yourself with that. We have other concerns that we must address," came the reply

"Tell us what we need to do, please?" He asked, sincerely.

Enosh seemed to have ignored the captain. He needed to consult with the others. He turned and headed into the edifice with the captain and his companions in tow. They were all rather curious as to what was going on. Enosh, then consulted with his companions. They were all sitting around a table conversing over things that seemed impossible, at least that was the ascertainment of the three. The vettigs were startled at the interruption. Then, Enosh, placed his hand upward, and Adama, placed his hand on Enosh's. Then the landing party witnessed a smile come over Adama's face as if to say he understood what was going on. There does seem to be a transfer of information in that brief moment. "Captain, give a few moments to consult with one another over this matter. In the meantime you can rest yourselves here," Adama said, pointing to the table. With that, the four vettigs went down the hallway of mystery. The captain and his entourage witnessed the bright lights, again. Just a few moments would pass before the vettigs would reunite themselves with the captain and his entourage.

"Captain, we want you to remain in orbit for a little bit. So, that we can formulate a plan to deal with this new concern. In the meantime, we wish to have the doctor and her husband as our guests. You may go back to your ship until you hear from us," said Abram.

"We will comply," the captain said. He knew that if, the doctor and the chief science officer were off the ship on the planet that they would safe. That would be two more people he would not have to worry about. Besides, being vettigs themselves they probably would know how to best proceed.

"But, captain, you need us on board, the ship" the science officer argued.

"Hal, I need your cooperation in all of this. It's vital to keep ourselves allied with these beings, here," the captain said, knowing that Hal would understand. There was a gentleness in his voice this time. It was one of concern.

The doctor turnd her husband around and looked eye to eye at him. There was a pleading in her countenance. She wanted her baby to be safe. And then he gave me in, nodding his head. "But, you' d better be careful, yourself, captain," he warned him. "I don't want to have to tell our baby his godfather died before he was born." The captain smiled and nodded. With that, the captain proceeded back to the ship.

Waiting was one of those things that the captain couldn't do very well. He was one of those people that needed to do something. Even, when he was trying to come up with the way to say his marriage proposal he still did something. Even though, it seemed like he wasn't.

CHAPTER 9

Back on Sol the wedding plans were on schedule. The only thing that was needed now was a date. That was still up in the air because of the mission that 'the stoic warrior' was on. Arna was rather concerned. She marched right into her father's office and demanded to know when her beloved was coming home. "Admiral, I'm here on a matter of utmost importance," she said, with consternation.

"Just a moment there, young lady, you don't come in here, especially, with that type of an attitude. I'm your father. And you will respect me!" He said with a great consternation in his voice.

"I'm sorry, Dad," she said pouting. Then she began to cry. "I'm just missing him so much. I need to know that he's okay."

The admiral came from behind his desk and brushed away the tears. "He's okay. I've been receiving reports on a regular basis," he said.

"Is he coming home? Is it going to be soon? I hope," she said sheepishly.

"Dry your eyes," he said, handing her a handkerchief. "We'll see what we can do." With that she seemed satisfied. She just needed reassurance. And dads are good for that. "In the meantime, I need you to help me with your mother. She's even more tenacious than you."

"I'll try. But you had better get him back here soon. Or I'll unleash her and Mother Gos both on you," she said, teasingly. She smiled. And that gave the admiral, a sigh of relief. After all, he was wondering what was going on, himself.

"Don't do that. I'll try my best. Please!" The admiral said, waving his hands in a riot. This made his daughter laugh. It was these human moments that made it all worthwhile.

"Admiral, the Emperor wishes to speak to you," Ms. Roy, his secretary informed him over the intercom.

"Put him on the screen," he ordered.

While, he was waiting for the screen to come on, the Emperor walked through the door. "Good morning, Admiral. And to you, too , Arna," he said, pleasantly.

The admiral came to attention and Arna stood up out of her seat. "I didn't know you were here," he said.

"Your , Majesty," Arna said, with a curtsy.

"Have you an update on..." the Emperor began to ask. He looked over as Arna curtsied again and left realizing that the Emperor was trying to be polite, but needed privacy.

"I'm sorry to say, I haven't, sire," the admiral said.

"When was the last time you heard from them?" He asked. "It's been a long time, hasn't it?"

"It sure has. Their scheduled updates have been a little irregular. The last update that they gave me was they were still investigating some complex issues concerning Eden and some vettigs. And that there were not quite clear on everything at this time," he replied to the Emperor.

"We'll just have to keep monitoring the communications grid," the Emperor said, and then turned to leave, "and pray that they are safe."

"My sentiments exactly," the admiral said, looking with concern at the Emperor. The Emperor understood the implications. The Emperor counted the captain as one of his friends. And in these days, friends counted for a lot for everyone. With that he turned and left.

Back at the home of the captain's parents, quite a different scene was happening. It seems that his father had taken a tumble off a ladder while trying to fix up one of the barns. With all the technology of the day he was more of a hands on kind of guy. "Al! Al! I'm coming!" His wife said excitedly, witnessing his fall.

"Roe, I'm all right," he told her as she came running over to him. Then he tried to stand up. "Ouch! I think I broke my foot."

"Honey, let me help you. Lean on me," she said with a sigh of relief, knowing that he could've done worse. She just shook her head as he threw his arm around her to lean on her. Then, she helped him inside. She called for a medic. Then she went over to the food synthesizer to get him some ice. She came back from the kitchen with a bag filled with ice and placed it on his foot to keep the swelling down. It didn't take the medic long to get there. With the technology of the day it only takes a few seconds to arrive not like the old days. Medical emergencies were the only way for translation devices to be used and were placed on a special setting to be used within the atmosphere. This made it far better for injured and sick parties to receive medical help. As soon as she placed the bag of ice on his foot the medic was there. He examined the foot and applied one of the hand held healing arrays to it. It was a matter of seconds that the pain left him. Then his foot just felt cold from the ice pack. "You can take the ice pack off now," the medic said. "He won't feel any pain anymore. But he should stay off it for a few hours to let the array take full effect. I'm giving you this healing array just in case something like this happens again. Its easy-to-use, just press this button. The foot should function normally, in fact, it should be better than it was before. Tell me, how did this happen? I need it for my report," the medic said.

As Al's wife, Roe, explained, the medic began to laugh. "Stay off ladders is my professional advice. Use one of your work drones for your menial tasks," he said.

"That's good advice," Al agreed.

Then while they were getting themselves settled, the doorbell rang. "Who is it now?" Said Roe as she opened the door. To her astonishment, it was her future daughter-in-law. She smiled and said, "come in." Her countenance became a little gentler.

"Mother Gos. I can call you that, can't I? I mean, we're almost related," she asked, hoping that she would say yes.

"Of course. That's okay. What can I do for you, sweetheart?" she said with a motherly tone putting Arna at ease.

"Good. I've just seen my father, and he is so patronizing. I mean, I'm his daughter and he should show me a little consideration," she said, sounding like a lamb baying for its mother.

"What's going on?" Al asked. "Is something up? That is that we don't know about?"

"No. It's just bureaucracy getting in the way," she replied. Then they understood what was going on. She was having an anxiety attack as most brides-to-be felt about this time. Mrs. Gos, knew all about this, remembering her own wedding. She then began to console her by putting her arms around her and giving her a big hug.

"Now, now, dear, I think that we can help. You just sit right there, sweetheart. I'll be right back," she told her. She went into the other room and brought out a cartridge to put into the entertainment center's video player. With that, they sat back and did what many people have done since the invention of the movie camera, they watched home movies.

The scene that the movie started with was that of Jay running around as a little boy. Everyone began to laugh and have a good time at the images they were watching. Jay would have been embarrassed. But this was a cathartic moment for everyone in the Gos house. "Get some popcorn out, you know we can't watch movies without popcorn. And get a few soft drinks as well," Al complained laughing the whole time, he said it. With that Roe went out into the dining area and did just that. This was what family was all about Arna. thought. She was glad she came.

Back on Eden, a different story was playing out. The vettigs had come back down the hallway after they had communed with the Grand Designer. The doctor and her husband were relieved. They weren't quite sure how long they would have had to wait. They were growing impatient.

"Adama, I would like to know why you wanted the privilege of our company. You know that we are needed on the ship," the science officer said.

"You're not as necessary, as you think. I mean, for up there. It is more important that we keep you and your lovely wife safe. The Grand Designer has informed us that your son will be instrumental in future events that we cannot give you the information on at this time. Suffice it to say, we're on a mission, right alongside you," Jess explained.

"That's fine. But we're getting a little anxious, not knowing what's going on," he replied.

"Well, we'll need to contact your captain, now. We have further orders to relate to him," Jess just informed the science officer. The science officer was curious about what was going on.

"You, mean to tell me that you've been in contact with the Grand Designer and he's real," the science officer replied, astonishingly.

"Now," Jess said, looking at him as though to say are you for real. The science officer chuckled to himself, realizing what he had just said. And who he had just said it to. What he learned from his studies of everything, this recent revelation of their power was hard to swallow. But there stood the vettigs, right there in front of him. And truth is truth.

"Why don't you tell me what's going on. Don't you think that we need to know?" The science officer asked. "After all, we are here at your invitation."

"Sit down, we'll tell you everything. Enosh, bring the good doctor over here, if you would, please," Jess said. "We're going to tell them all about it."

With that, Jess and the good doctor came over to the table. The doctor sat down with her husband. And then Jess began the explanation. The two listening, were informed of the importance of their baby. "Well, it says in the Book of Prophecies in the New Tribute, that there will be a herald that will usher in a new dawn for all of humanity. This period of time will be called the Golden Age of the Grand Designer. And then, all of humanity will be changed at the end of that time period. Then they will live going between this galaxy and the Kingdom of Light. Then all of mankind will live throughout eternity. And the Herald is crucial to this plan."

"So you mean, our son will be that Herald?" The doctor asked.

"Not exactly. Your son will be the ancestor to the Herald. It is through this son that he will come. This is what the Grand Designer has told us," Jess informed them.

"So that's why you wanted us to be with you? You wanted us to be safe," the science officer said.

"Exactly! We want to make sure that the Grand Designer's plan went into effect without any problems. And we can best protect you down here than up there on your ship," he explained.

"What makes you think that they are coming? You know, the captain left him arguing with the other vettig," the science officer said.

"No matter how intense the argument between the two they would have never let you go. They would have restrained you first. They intended to let you go. It's just a matter of how long it will be before they get here. They may have been arguing just to make you think that you had the upper hand. But, I sense that it might not be too much longer," Abram said as he joined the entourage. With that everyone became quiet. They just listened. What they were listening for, the doctor and the science officer wasn't quite for sure.

Up, on the ship there was a different story playing out. General quarters had been sounded. Everyone was at their duty station. The captain and crew were on high alert. The sensors had detected some sort of anomaly, something that they had never seen before. They weren't quite for sure what it was. But, they felt that it could be of a danger to everyone concerned. The anomaly did not move, nor did it have the signature of a quantum stream. It was like nothing that they had ever seen before.

The colonel had made it back to the home world of the Union, Rama, to file his report. As he entered into the inner chambers of the consulate. He was surprised to see a stranger standing at the side of the Prime Minister. The stranger said nothing, but the Prime Minister ordered him to give his report.

"Prime Minister, I wish to report a grave emergency. We may be under attack by some factions unknown. And it could happen at any time," the colonel explained.

"Highly, unlikely," came the reply. "This is an emissary from a good friend of the Union. You may know him as Beil. He informs me that they are looking out for our interests." The person behind the Prime Minister remained a mystery.

The colonel was astonished. It was the first time that the prime minister ever saw him with his mouth open. It made to Prime Minister chuckle.

"By your leave, sir," the colonel said, bowing his head in respect.

"You may go," he said, waving his hand up and down, to indicate he was done with him. "Remember to keep me updated as to how everything is going." He said looking at his subordinate, then he began to smile. With that, the mysterious stranger left.

The colonel went back to his ship. He then began to set up , at least for the Star Blaster defense mechanisms. He wanted to be ready just in case they were to be attacked. After all, he was the one instrumental in helping the Nova to escape from Beil's planet. He could be considered an enemy in his way of thinking. Then it happened, the mysterious ship that they had gotten the oddball signature from was at Rama. The colonel sounded general quarters and everybody took their duty stations. "There is a transmission coming in, colonel," the comm-officer said.

"Put it through," came the order.

"Colonel, there's no need to call general quarters. Stand down," the voice ordered.

"Who sent that message?" The colonel asked.

"The other ship," came the reply.

"Did we register anything other than the message from the other ship?" The colonel asked puzzled.

"No, sir, we didn't," the X0 replied. "Not until they were on top of us."

"Then how did they know we were at general quarters?" He asked, still puzzled. Then the voice registered, it was Beil. "Send transmission! We are standing down. But, we will stay on high alert. Send that," he ordered.

Back at Eden a new scenario was transpiring. A ship just arrived. It was similar to the ships that they had encountered before. This time, the Nova was ready. Then, they were being haled by the other ship. It was a different sounding voice. "Nova, we are here to assist you. Let us know if there is anything we can do. We will be contacting the others on the surface. And we will be setting up a base planet side," the voice said.

The captain thought to himself with all this hardware who could come against them and win. "We welcome the help. Please, let us know if we can help you in anyway," he said. He sensed a type of peace about the whole situation.

Planet side, there was a sigh of relief, because they had been monitoring the transmissions.

Evidently, there were others that sensed the need. "We have the upper hand now. I wonder what the enemy is thinking?" Adama said thinking out loud. He wasn't sensing anything at this time. He knew that Luus had tremendous power and could cloak himself, even from his fellow vettigs. It was about that time that something happened, a displacement in a part of space just outside a typical orbit of the planet. Then a ship appeared. It was the elusive Luus. But, little did they know he had picked up some help along the way. These were the creatures of darkness, alluded to in the Books of History in the Holy Chronicles. Creatures of darkness were lesser beings that had certain powers created by Luus causing the common person to think they were more than what they were. Their mysteriousness was their greatest asset in making people think that. It seemed like that this would be quite a battle. And that blood might be shed.

"Open a frequency to the surface. We need to see if they are seeing what we are seeing," the captain ordered.

"Adama, are you seeing, what we are seeing?" Asked the captain.

"Yes, captain, we are and more so. Just stay where you are. Our ship will be docking with yours. If you will allow them to do so," Adama said. "They can place a shield about both themselves and you, that will protect you from their weapons and any other strategy that they could come up with."

"We welcome the assist," he replied. With that they began their defense. A field went up around the ship when Luus's ship began its assault on the Nova. Allowing a stronger field to go up around the planet. After a few moments of bombardment on the ship with no results they turned their attentions toward the planet. They began to see that their efforts were to no avail. The field of energy that was placed around both the ships and the planet held up. On the ship that was bombarding the planet, Luus began barking out orders. One of the creatures turned to inform him that it was to no avail. Then he ordered, "let's get out of here. We can come back on another day when they aren't so prepared." And with that the Nova watched as they saw them go out of sight.

"XO, keep the long-range scanners going as long as you can. They might come back," the captain ordered. He was erring on the cautious side. The rest of the ship was relieved and thought that they had won a victory. The captain could hear cheers from throughout the ship. But he knew better than anyone else that they were far from victorious. "Open a transmission to the planet."

"Captain, I have Adama for you," the communications officer replied.

"On screen!" The captain said. He turned his attention to the screen in front of him as the image appeared. "Adama, how is everything down there?"

"Everything is just fine. I see that it's the same up there," came the reply. "Now, captain, we need for you to come down so that we can give you further strategies."

"I'll be right there as soon as I can get to the translator room," the captain replied. "XO, you have the ship. Keep watching those scanners." With that, he headed to the translation room.

Once he was planet side, he went to the edifice where everyone was waiting. As he entered the room, "how is everyone doing?" He asked.

"Everyone is fine, captain. What are your orders?" The science officer asked.

"That's up to Adama, and his friends. We're not out of the woods yet. They may come back," the captain said, as a matter of fact.

"We feel that they will not come back, at least not for a while. We are in no danger here on Eden. But, if they catch you away from here, you may be. So, this is what we are going to do. We're going to help you get back to your home planet," Jess said.

"Thank you, for your help. We feel that we can trust all of you," the captain said with genuine gratitude in his demeanor.

"But, what about us? What are we supposed to do?" The good doctor asked. With that the vettig's smiled. Then each one placed their right hand on her stomach closed their eyes and started to speak in an unknown language. Oddly, the doctor was at peace about the whole thing. It seemed she was understanding everything that they said. Hearing a language that had never been spoken before she was amazed. When they were done, her husband looked at her with questions written across his face. "They blessed our baby and they prophesied over him. Didn't you understand what they were saying?" She replied to the looks on his face.

"No I didn't," he replied. "It was a strange language. A language I've never heard."

"I'm sorry. The language we used was an ancient language. I guess you would call it a dead language. But we vettigs still use it," Enosh explained. "We were blessing the baby. What we said was that he would grow up to be a strong, intelligent leader among his people." The science officer smiled and began to strut around like a male royal barn bird. Everyone began to laugh.

"We must be going then. Time waits for no man. I learned that a long time ago," the captain said. With that, they headed back to the ship. As they arrived, the science officer couldn't keep from smiling. His wife, just watched as she saw her husband exhibiting emotions she had never seen him exhibit before. Her thoughts were he's more like a typical man than he wants everyone to know. As the science officer and the captain arrived on the bridge, the captain started ordering everyone to stand down from general quarters. But, he ordered a modified yellow alert.

"What happened down there?" The XO asked.

"Nothing of consequence," came the reply. "We need to get back to Sol. There's a matter that we need to discuss with the Emperor." The captain was trying to think of what he would say to him when he got there.

"Course is laid in, captain," the navigator responded.

"Steady as she goes, helmsman, we want to get there in one piece. The other ship will be tagging along," the captain told them. They had already separated from the other ship. The vettig on board the other ship haled the Nova. " This is the Star Keeper, and we wish to inform, you, that we will be accompanying you all the way," he said.

"What's your name?" The captain asked.

"My name is Mischa," came the reply. "If there's anything that you need just feel free to call. We try not to stand on ceremony."

"Thank you, Mischa. We'll try to remember that," the captain said. With that the sister ships headed back towards the heart of the Empire. The captain was looking forward to getting back. He had several reasons why he wanted to get back. The first and foremost was to encounter the Emperor. Then, it was to get together with his 'little pixie'. There was so much information that needed to be exchanged, he was glad that there was more than himself, to help in the explaining of things. He knew that the computer recorded quite a bit of the information for them, that would help. He had the science officer put the messages from the two evil vettigs into the computer. He also had four copies of the messages made. One for himself and the other three went to his inner circle, the 'brain trust'. He felt safer that way. As they kept their course, they still kept the long-range scanners going. The hair on the back of the captain's neck was still standing up. He was still wondering if somewhere out there watching. A communiqué was sent informing Imperial Command of their impending arrival and their need to have an audience with the Emperor. It gave the names of all who would be attending this special audience, including Mischa. The message was sent out after consulting with Mischa and asking him if he would accompany them to the surface of Sol. He knew this was a request and hoped that the Emperor would grant it. Mischa had assured them that he would. His feelings were that the Emperor would be more forthcoming with him along. The captain concurred.

"As we enter the orbit, gentlemen, we will be taking a defensive posture. Protecting the home planet is first and foremost," the captain ordered. With that everyone on the bridge nodded their heads in agreement. They continued on course to accomplish their mission. "Get me Mischa on the horn."

"Mischa here, captain," he said as his image was projected on the screen on the arm of the captain's chair.

"Mischa, is there any thing else that we need to do before we get to the planet?" The captain asked.

"No there isn't. But when we get there I feel that we need to dock our ships together again. That way I can press the automatic defensive shield that we used back at Eden," he said.

"That will be fine," came the captain's reply. The captain thought that that would be one less thing he would have to worry about, his crew would be safe.

As they approached the planet and began their orbits. Then the Mischa joined them on the Nova after they joined their ships. This would allow for them to go to the surface together. As they docked at the shuttle bay near the palace they were discussing their strategy. How would they explain everything. They found themselves entering into the great Hall still discussing this not realizing their departure from the shuttle. Everyone had a lot of questions on their minds. The only one that seemed in the know was Mischa. The captain chuckled to himself of the lunacy of the occasion. Then they found themselves right in front of the Emperor, sitting on his throne. The Emperor looked uncomfortable. As if he knew what was coming. "Gentlemen, and Lady, why have you asked for this audience?" The Emperor asked.

"We have a matter of grave importance that we need to discuss with you. We are still on our mission to investigate the event that we all know started this whole mess," replied the captain being the speaker of the group.

"Explain yourself," the Emperor said with a stoic manner about himself. He wasn't about to let them know his thoughts.

They all started to talk at one time. After a few moments of this, the Emperor held his hand up to stop the proceedings. They all just froze. If the matter wasn't so serious, the Emperor might have laughed at the whole proceeding. But as it was, he maintained his composure. "Not everyone at one time. Captain, you be the spokesperson for the group. If you would, please?" The Emperor graciously requested.

"Well it started on a mysterious planet and has ended up here. We have found the truth. I mean the truth about the vettigs. Evidently, this is been a secret for quite some time. Our question to you is, did you know about it?" The captain was trying to be clear as he could. He didn't wanted to put the Emperor on the spot with way out.

"If you're asking did I know about vettigs being the Messengers of Light, I did," the Emperor said, perceiving their thoughts. "This knowledge has been handed down from Emperor to Emperor for generations. Only the Emperor and his immediate family is supposed to know the truth. It has been a rule written down in the Book of Emperors for generations as well. They have discretionary power over things like that, we will call it above top secret, only on a need to know basis."

"So, you're saying that you knew. What else do you know about the situation?" The captain asked surprised by the Emperor's honesty.

"Well, I do know a lot of the passages of the Holy Chronicles that refer to these Messengers of Light. I also know that the word vettig is from an ancient language that is no longer spoken. Its meaning is one with light. I believe that is a literal translation. What do you say, my friend?" The Emperor said, directing his gaze at the vettig that had accompanied the crew of the Nova.

"Yes, Sire, I believe so. And by the way my name is Mischa. I have been sent here to be a consultant and an emissary on the matter at hand from the Council of Messengers. And we will be advising you as things go along," he explained.

"Thank you, for your indulgence in our petty squabbles. I am so humbled by your presence," the Emperor said bowing his head to the vettig.

Everyone in the Hall was amazed and fascinated at the Emperor's attitude. "Sire, we need to formulate a strategy as to how to proceed next. What I'm asking is, what should we do?" The captain asked.

"We'll bow to the expert, Mischa," the Emperor replied. "We need to have a strategy of some sort. It would mean so much to me and my people if we could bring everything to light. What are your thoughts?"

"The Council has sent me to ascertain what's going on, and then to relate to them, everything that I have learned. But, I am to proceed at my own discretion," he replied.

With that, there was a moment of silence in the Great Hall. It was the good doctor that broke the silence. "Well, one thing I do know for sure is that we need to defend ourselves at all cost," she said.

"I believe that the information about the vettigs should be shared with your military. But, there needs to be a discretionary clause in the giving out of this information. I feel that the joint chief's of staff should know. And all commanders of military ships should be informed. We will give the discretionary clause as top-secret need-to-know. Would that be satisfactory with you?" The Emperor said, bowing to Mischa.

"That will be fine. This way, we can still keep a low profile and aid humanity," Mischa said in agreement. As soon he finished his statement there was an alarm sounded.

"What's going on? Get a hold of my advisers," the Emperor said.

"Commander, what's going on up there?" The captain asked pressing the buttons on his communicator.

"Sir, there have been several ships that have placed themselves in orbit around the planet. We are trying to hale them at this moment," the communication officer replied.

"What's happening, mister?" The captain asked. Waiting on the lieutenant commander to reply to his inquiry.

"They're not hostile. They are our allies," the communication officer replied, with relief. "They are wanting to know if they could come planet side to consult with you down there."

"Well, Emperor, what do you say?" The captain asked.

"Tell them to proceed," the Emperor said. "And, captain, I'll need your expertise. And of course your 'brain trust' as well." He smiled, having heard that term before, during one of his many conversations with the captain.

The captain beamed with pride pointing at those he brought with him. "We'll be happy to help," he said. "But, I think that we still have a lot to do. I think that this investigation is far from being over. If, you understand what I mean."

"Yes, I do. There is something else that needs attention, besides this. If I'm understanding everything, you're about to engage in a wedding ceremony sometime soon. Aren't you?" The Emperor asked.

The captain had almost forgotten about the whole matter. He turned to the Emperor and bowed. Without saying a word he took his leave to go see his 'little pixie'. With that, he rushed out of the great Hall, realizing he didn't have transportation to get him to where he needed to go. When all of a sudden the royal limo pulled up. The driver said, "compliments of the Emperor." With a big smile on his face he opened the rear door and got in. The captain couldn't look a gift horse in the mouth, fortune was smiling down on him.

"Make a rush of it, please," he said, anxiously.

He was finally going to be able to set sort of a date with his beloved. He had left everybody else to fend for themselves. He was on a mission that was on a need-to-know basis, he chuckled to himself. He figured that with all the help that arrived he could have some personal moments to himself. As the limo headed up the lane that was near the admiral's home Jay was getting anxious. He had ascertained from his conversation with his driver that Arna was at her parents' home.

Inside the home Arna's mother saw the official seal on the plates of the limo. She started to get flustered. She wanted to make sure her hair was done just right seeing it was a mess in the mirror, then she looked at her clothes. She didn't have time to change. There was no way she could look presentable enough for the Emperor in as little time as she had. She kept looking out the window and calling to her daughter. Her daughter was in one of the back rooms, tidying up. Then she saw him. She started to laugh to herself, it was her future son-in-law. She said to herself, "I wonder how he got that. Only, Jay. Only, Jay." She shook her head and opened the door. She gave a real big smile as he came running up to her.

"Where's Arna? There's something we need to discuss," he said.

"Arna! Arna! Get yourself out here! Someone is here to see you," she yelled with enthusiasm.

Arna came out from the back looking up from brushing her hands off, she saw him. She ran and leaped into his arms, he spun her around while they kissed. Her mother, quietly bowed out and went into the kitchen. "What are you doing here? I didn't realize that the Nova had arrived," she said with a questioning look Jay had seen before.

"I went AWOL," he said with a smile.

"Stop teasing," she said hitting him on the shoulder.

"That hurt. But it was a good hurt," he said. "Come over here. Sit down with me to talk about..." And they seated themselves on the couch. Then all of a sudden from the kitchen came, her mother.

"Jay, I just received a message from headquarters, we're supposed to check in in person," she said with a look of dread on her face interrupting them. "I believe we are at war."

"What do you mean, at war?" The captain Jay asked. With that, the realization that something was up hit him. "The limo and the driver are at my disposal, all day. Let's go." With that, they all left and went back to the Military Citadel.

"Sir, I've just received a communiqué. I'm to take you with the ladies back. I'm supposed to drop them off at the Citadel and then proceed onto the palace with you. There'll be somebody there to meet the ladies," the driver said.

"Did they tell you anything else?" The admiral's wife asked.

"That's all I know, ma'am. I'm just supposed to take you two to the Citadel and him to the palace," he replied.

As everyone was wondering what was going on, the captain began to finish what he was going to say back at the house. "Arna, when this whole thing is over. I don't care when it is. We're going to get married. So prepare yourself for a quick wedding. And don't worry about, who is going to officiate. I'll see to that," he said. He didn't have a clue as to whom it was going to be.

"Anything, you want. As long as we are together and married. It's all right with me," she replied. Her mother began to cry. "Mom, what are you crying for?"

"I'm just so happy," she replied. Then Arna began to cry right along with her. Jay just shrugged his shoulders not knowing what to do. The driver chuckled to himself.

"I guess it doesn't make any difference what station of life here you're in, your humanism will always come out," the driver said to himself as he proceeded to complete his mission. Then the captain sat back and began to wonder, what was up. Was there something else that they were missing. Could the two elusive vettigs have formed an alliance with the Union. Or was it something else.

CHAPTER 10

J ust before the message was sent to the admiral's house.
The myriad of ships orbiting the planet had increased in
number and filling the space around the Nova. As the Nova
was watching the space around them fill up they were glad that
this armada was on their side. The captain was oblivious to all
the new elements developing. The navigator issued the order to
hale the other ships trying to make some sort of sense of it all.
"Haling! No answer! Haling again! Sir, I believe somebody is
wanting to talk to us," the communication officer said, puzzled
by not being able to locate where it was coming from.

"On screen!" The navigator ordered being put in charge by
the captain, making him the duty officer.

"To whom am I speaking?" The figure on the screen
asked.

"My name is Lieutenant Roe. To whom am I speaking?
You look familiar," he said, perplexed. Turning his head from
side to side as if he were sizing him up and trying to remember
where he saw him. His face looked so familiar to him.

"I'm the Grand Vettig Jehu," he said with a smile.

"Your Holiness, I thought I recognized you. You look just like your pictures. How may we be of assistance to you?" The lieutenant asked.

"I understand that you have been investigating a particular event. We've been keeping tabs on everything that has been going on," he explained, sounding rather proper. "We would like to speak to your captain, is he available."

"No, sir, but we can get a hold of him. He's on the planet down below," he replied.

"That will be all right. I'm already on the planet. We'll ask for him to come to see us from wherever he is," the Grand Vettig said not knowing the order had already gone out.

The navigator was so impressed with the politeness that a man of his stature had, bowing down to somebody like himself. That was the type of man, that somebody could get to know and feel good about following.

As the communication officer on the planet relayed a message to relayed the Grand Vettig about contacting the captain he was pleased. The Emperor found himself hosting the Grand Vettig, and his entourage. A special frequency was set up for the Grand Vettig to keep in contact with his ever growing armada. The Emperor made sure are thing was set into motion in the proper manner. His own people was to keep him alerted if anything went wrong. "Sire, is there anything else that we can do for you?" His secretary inquired.

"No, there isn't. I'm going to wait would the Grand Vettig on the captain," he replied.

"I'll be in my office if you need me. Just call me, whatever it might be," Ms. Rae said.

The Grand Vettig was amiable. The Emperor was so glad that everything was that the Grand Vettig had arrived. He also felt relieved to know that the Grand Vettig was apprised of the incident that had happened several days ago, the event that started this whole thing. It amazed him how nothing got by him.

"We knew that this day would come. We have been preparing for it. Not knowing when it would come. But, we are prepared for it," the vettig explained.

"Then what should we be doing?" The Emperor asked.

"Well, we'll do everything together from here on out. Our concern is not that they learned about our secret, but rather dealing with the root cause of the revelation of it. Mainly, the two, that started this whole thing. Their aim was to disgrace the Grand Designer. But, we will deal with them," the Grand Vettig.

The captain found himself perplexed as they dropped the ladies off at the Citadel. He was wondering if it was the worst-case scenario. After all the rogue vettigs seemed to be on the side of the Union. He would know more when he got there.

Arna and her mother were greatly concerned with the possibility of war. It didn't seem to take them that long to make it to the admiral's office. "Is he in?" The admiral's wife asked with a grave tone in her voice.

"Yes, ma'am, he is. Go right on in. He's expecting you," the secretary replied.

"Arn, what's going on? Are we at war?" She asked him. "You know, we have no secrets."

"No, sweetheart, we're not at war. But I needed the two of you to be here to explain what is about to happen. I didn't mean to be so cryptic over the communication frequencies. Just please be open minded," he replied, trying to explain himself.

"Open minded?" His daughter quizzed him.

"The Grand Vettig is here. And for lack of better words, has asked your captain and the Nova to do, what may seem to be a suicide mission to me. Without going into details at this time with you, I thought that you needed to know what lie ahead. If I know Jay, as I do. He'll do it. He's that type of man," the admiral explained, not knowing what the whole thing was about, himself.

"But, Dad, what are you talking about?" Arna asked.

"I'm sorry that I am not very clear. Let me start from the beginning. Approximately, 3 to 4 weeks ago there was an event, a catastrophic event, a moon exploded at a planet that was nearby, Vashti. We sent the Nova to investigate. It was during this investigation that certain top-secret, need-to-know things were brought to light. Because of this, we now find ourselves facing an enemy that we really know nothing about. And it is up to the crew of the Nova to place itself in harms way. But, the Emperor and the Grand Vettig both felt that it should be a voluntary mission. And they authorized me to tell the two of you, because of your personal involvement with Jay. There are some security people bringing in his parents so that I could speak with them personally about the same manner," the admiral explained.

"But, what does the Grand Vettig have to do with all this?" The admiral's wife asked.

"That's a part of the top-secret, need-to-know things that I was alluding to," he explained. "All we can do is pray. And hope that all goes well. I don't believe that it is a suicide mission, but there is an element of danger," he was trying to be hopeful telling them these things. He still thought in the back of his mind it was a suicide mission. He was trying to do a low backpedaling to his previous statement.

"Sweetheart, I'll keep praying. In fact, I've been trying ever since I received your communiqué about all this back at the house," the admiral's wife said.

Back at the great Hall the Emperor was laying out the plan. He told the captain and the others that if they could use their ship as a decoy, that there might be a possibility of capturing the two rogues. But, he wanted it to be a voluntary mission. The Grand Vettig had been in complete agreement with the whole thing. The captain was pleased to know that everyone had their best interests at heart.

"I'll have to present this to my ship. This is one time when, I believe everyone needs to have a vote," the captain said. "When I told everyone that it was a dictatorship in the military, I never knew that things like this would happen."

"I know what you mean. That's why I couldn't order you myself," the Emperor replied. "Take as much time as you need to come up with the decision."

"This is something that I can't just put out over the communication link. I want to go back to the ship is presented in person. If that's all right with you, Sire?" The captain asked. "We'll send you our answer and then take it from there."

"You have your leave," the Emperor said, solemnly. With that the entourage that came with the captain went back to the ship. On the trip back up to the ship, there was silence. It seemed like everyone was actually praying for this one.

"Captain, I think I have a solution. But, I'll need a little time to formulate the right words," the doctor said, breaking the silence just before they landed in the shuttle bay.

"All right, doctor, let me know what you've got. Anything, anything at all that could help," the captain said.

As they left the shuttle the captain went to the bridge to make his announcement. The others, except for the good doctor, were with him. The doctor went to her sick bay to check with everyone there as the announcement came. "We have been chosen for a vital mission that, may cause great harm to us and to our ship. I'm asking for a vote. I cannot order you to put your lives in jeopardy. Therefore, I need everyone to put a vote on the nearest comm-panel. Vote yea or nay. The computer will tabulate the results and get them to me," he explained. He knew that it would take a little while for this process to be completed.

"Captain, I think I have figured out what I needed to say, but, I need to go back down to the planet and discuss it with the grand vettig. If that's all right with you, sir," the doctor said piping in on the communication panel at sick bay.

"Okay, go ahead. Do what you thinks best, and by the time you get there we'll have the results," came the captain's reply. With that, she headed back to the shuttle bay taking one of the smaller shuttles to the surface.

The results came in, it was unanimous for doing the mission. The captain smiled as if he knew that that was going to be the result. He had the best crew in the fleet. Then his thoughts turned toward what should we do. Or rather, where should we go to complete this mission. Then he realized he needed to tell the Emperor the results. The captain gave the order to the communications officer to open a frequency to the planet down below and route it to his captain's chair. As the screen, in the arm of his chair lit up to give him a little more privacy than the bridge view-screen would have he saw the Emperor with the Grand Vettig. "Gentlemen, we have a unanimous vote. What are your orders?" The captain reported.

"Go back to the planet, where you first encountered Beil. Then just wait there. My ships shall be in the area to give you the assistance that you need. The hardest part of this is the waiting," the Grand Vettig replied. "We vettigs know how to wait. It's a part of our design. But you humans, that's a different matter altogether."

"Understandable. We humans weren't designed that way. But it's your show, we'll do it your way," the captain said being condescending. "Gos out. Helmsman take us back to Beil's planet. We'll wait there."

With that they began the journey back to the planet mentioned. This would be a very tricky matter, because it was on the other side of the Titanium Barrier. Not only did they have to watch out for the two rogue vettigs, but they also had to watch out for Union ships as well. The captain knew that he would be in violation of the treaty. But he felt confident in the fact that the vettigs would be behind him in everything that he did from here on out. After all, he was helping them clean up their own backyard, so to speak.

Nobody noticed that the doctor had not come back from her trip to Sol. She was with the vettigs. She had gone to the Grand Vettig and told him of her vision. Unknown to the captain they had decided to have her accompany them. The interpretation of her vision gave them the idea to place a good vettig on the world were a rogue vettig was banished. This idea was the strategy they needed to ensure the Grand Designer's plan. After the capture of these two this strategy would be put into place. The Grand Vettig was astonished at the fact that the Grand Designer had given her such insight about this whole ordeal. But in the midst of their conversation he realize who she was. It would be her descendant that would be the

Herald of the Golden Age. This would explain a lot. This was the teaching that the Kingdom of Light would become a part of this reality. So why why wouldn't the Grand Designer, give her such insight. It would be an age that would never end. The Kingdom would rule from that point throughout eternity. But this kingdom would come after a period of time in the galaxy's future. There was still the Dark Decade to come. This would be a 10 year period , where the two vettigs would be given a chance to be in control. But all this was yet to come. The Grand Designer knew this. That is why he interfered with their plans. Some didn't even know he was doing such things. The teaching of the Grand Designer had been diluted over the years. Some things had gone to the wayside do to lack of interest by the people. Therefore, there were inaccuracies in the teachings being taught today. And there were other teachings that had gotten lost over the years as well. But, there were some that had kept up with the truth. This is one of the reasons why the vettigs were designed to be of a benefit to humanity, to teach the truth.

As the Nova headed for its destination, the science officer realized his wife wasn't aboard. "Captain, have you seen Joy? I don't think she came back to the ship after she had gone down to the planet. I hope everything is okay?" Hal said.

"If, she's still back on the planet. Then she will be out of harms way. That'll be one less headache to worry about. Do you understand?" The captain replied. Hal nodded his head, agreeing with the captain. He sighed a sigh of relief, realizing that not only was she out of harms way. So was his baby. Neither one of them knew she was with the Grand Vettig.

As the Nova approached the planet, they set up their orbit. It was a routine matter. Now the hardest part, waiting. Everyone went about their duties as normal, but they were on high alert. The captain watched as everyone was at their wits end, waiting. The captain, however, stayed calm. He wanted to put on an air of confidence to keep morale high. But inside he was feeling something altogether different. He was thinking about back home, his parents, their farm, and his 'little pixie'. He hoped that all his plans for the future would come to fruition. The ship was on that modified port and starboard duty again.

It'd been several days when something happened. There was three ships that approached the planet. As their instruments having been calibrated to detect them indicated. The captain wondered who this third party was and where did they come from? Then the thought, can we pull this off? As this last thought went through the captain's head they were haled by Luus's ship. "Captain, you've come back to us. We got off on the wrong foot the last time. Let's make amends. We can get together on the surface and break bread together. Does that sound like a good idea?" Luus said.

"We can get together, as you wish. But, I request that it be only you and I. If that will be all right with you?" The captain replied.

"I agree. I'll meet you down there. Luus out!" he said.

"Pappy, you have the ship. I'll be back soon," the captain ordered. The XO was ready to give his arguments as to why the captain should not be going alone. When the captain raised his hand as if to say, I don't want to hear it. Then the XO slinked back in frustration knowing that his words would have fallen on deaf ears. The captain was his superior officer. He headed towards the translation room to proceed down to the planet.

On the planet there again he saw the edifice that was there before. This made him wonder how such a thing could happen.

Was this a part of the power that the vettigs had. Could they summon up such things at will. And how did they transport themselves to the surface without anyone catching it on a scanning array. They were fortunate that they could calibrate their scanners to detect their ships. The scanning arrays were among the most sophisticated and sensitive pieces of equipment that the ship had. They should have detected when the vettigs left their ships, but didn't. As Luus approached the captain from the edifice, he smiled. "My good captain. I am so pleased to see you again. It has been a while since we've seen each other and I want to offer you some refreshments," he said.

"Lead the way," the captain replied. It was his show. The captain was being very cautious about this whole encounter. He knew that he was in the presence of a powerful being. "The table looks like it's set for a king." He was trying to humor him playing for time. Knowing that the trap would be sprung at any moment.

"Is that what you would like to be, a king?" He asked. Trying to get a read on the captain, so he could manipulate the situation to his advantage.

"Not really. I like my life the way it is. But on a different subject, why are we here ?" He asked.

"Well... see captain... I want us to be friends. We shouldn't be at each other's throat. We should be allying ourselves with one another to spread the truth," Luus said.

"The truth. What is the truth?" the captain asked .

"The truth is a matter of interpretation. You see, we can do anything we want with the truth," he replied.

"That sounds like a lie to me," he said.

"No it's not a lie. It is an interpretation," he replied smiling like a Cheshire cat.

"I guess I'm too honest for you. I prefer the real truth. The real truth is, is that you are a fake, a limited being," he said. "Isn't that true?"

"Captain, you don't know what you're saying," the vettig said gritting his teeth. Getting ready to pounce.

"Well, I think I do. I've read the Holy Chronicles for myself. And what it said was very plain to me. You are a limited being. Of course you have power, the type of power that could wipe me out right now. But, you would only be wiping out my body, not my soul. And I would gladly give up my body for the principle of truth. So do what you will, I won't change my mind," the captain spoke confidently. When he was through with his speech, the vettig raised his hand. Then he found he couldn't do anything. This put a scare into him. And it made the captain wonder what was going on at this time. The captain began to use hand to hand combat and was winning. The captain wondered why such a thing could happen. But he wasn't looking a gift horse in the mouth. The battle didn't last long and the vettig was defeated.

"Captain, you think you may have defeated me here, but there is another front, where you cannot. I give you leave to contact your ship," he said, breathing hard from the defeat. But feeling rather smug, thinking there was an eminent defeat in space, by his tiny armada.

"Pappy, what's going on up there?" The captain said pressing the buttons on the communicator around his neck.

"We're under attack. We have shields up. We can't get to you right now. We'll let you know what's going on in a little bit," the XO replied.

"Keep the ship, safe. That's your orders. I'm all right at this time," the captain said.

"You may have defeated me down here, but, up there, I'll win," he laughed taunting him.

"That's all right, we have a plan. Just watch and learn," the captain replied. With that he realized that the battle was almost over. The vettig was watching his defeat.

"Captain, let's be reasonable. I can get you anything you want. Please, help me," Luus said. Realizing his demise was inevitable.

"You don't understand. I don't need your type of help. Neither does man kind. We are doing fine without you. Besides, I have everything I want," the captain replied being a little smug himself. He was referring to everything back home.

With that, it seemed like everything was frozen in time. Then the space around the Nova became bright. Then it filled up with ships. This was the plan to swoop in at the last moment and save the day. The Grand Vettig timed it just right. They had captured the rogue vettigs. The Nova gave a sigh of relief at the sight. "Well, I'll be. Could they have been more dramatic?" The XO said.

"Is everyone over there okay," the Grand Vettig said as he opened a frequency to the Nova.

"We're all fine. We thank you for coming to our rescue. The captain is on the surface, awaiting the outcome," the communications officer replied. There was relief in his voice.

"It was my pleasure. We needed to get a handle on those vettigs, so I thank you for your participation. Please, allow me to congratulate the captain, in my own way," the Grand Vettig said. With that he went to the surface of the planet to meet with the captain and the rogue vettig.

The other vettig with his minions were already taken into custody. On the surface, the Grand Vettig found a most unusual scene. There was the captain, who was sitting there on a tree stump watching Luus. He began to chuckle to himself as he saw the sight. "Why, captain, you have everything well in hand, I see."

"It wasn't hard. He's just a little kitty cat," the captain replied with a big smile on his face. "It seems that when you vettigs are in your corporeal state that you're no stronger than we are. But, he was about to use some sort of power on me but couldn't. Was that your doing?"

"No, captain, it was someone else," he replied. Pointing up as if to say, the Grand Designer had something to do with it.

"Someone else, eh?" He said looking up the word feigning thoughtfulness.

"Need I say more," he said with a gleam in his eye. The captain kind of shrugged his shoulders as if to say, who me? Why am I so special? Understanding will thing.

"We need to get them somewhere where everybody could be safe. So what's your plan?" The captain said.

"Well, it exactly wasn't my plan. It was something that the doctor came up with, she had this vision. She told me all about it and that she didn't tell anybody else for fear that it might be something other than what it was. We're going to place them back on the planets that they escaped from. But this time, we are going to place a vettig, a good vettig to guard them," he explained.

"Does that mean the doctor is with you , then?" The captain asked.

"How intuitive of you. Yes, the doctor is with me, or at least on my ship," he replied. The captain just stood there. The Grand Vettig noticed that the captain had something else on his mind. "Was there something else that I could help you with?"

"Well, sir, I was wondering if you could help me with little matter," the captain said.

"After all, you have done for us, as well as the galaxy, nothing is too little of a matter," replied the Grand Vettig.

"I'm engaged to be married. I was wondering if... you could possibly see fit to... officiate the wedding?" The captain fumbled in his question.

"I would be happy to," he replied with a smile.

The captain felt that his fiancée would be surprised to see such a distinguished person officiating their wedding. It would give him quite a few bonus points for their wedding night. The captain began to smile and strut around as if he had done something great. In fact he had. He had saved the galaxy from two megalomaniacs. And had gotten the reclusive Grand Vettig to officiate his wedding. Not to mention that he had kept his promise to Arna. Any announcements or speeches or sermons of the Grand Vettig were usually taped ahead of time and then released in a timely manner giving him the time needed to do this. The captain knew kept strutting. The

Grand Vettig laughed with the captain. Then the captain came to himself realizing he needed to contact his ship. "Pappy, is everything okay up there?" He asked, via his communicator.

"Everything is A-OK. It seems that the cavalry arrived just in time. It is over? Is it really over?" The XO said.

"Not really. We have one more thing that we need to do," came the captain's reply. "Get the ship ready were heading back. Is that understood?"

"Aye! Aye! Captain," he replied. "It is soon as you get here, we can go."

The Grand Vettig nodded at the captain, telling him he would be there. They smiled at each other and went their separate ways. The elusive vettigs were caught. The third ship was a ship filled with their minions. Everyone could be dealt with appropriately. Jehu, the Grand Vettig gave charge to several of the other vettigs to do the imprisonment. Then he headed toward Sol. He was looking forward to officiating the wedding. Usually, the only weddings, he officiated were Imperial weddings. This would be a pleasant change for him.

CHAPTER 11

As the entourage of ships headed back to the planet, Sol, a message was sent back to the Imperial Fleet Command. All it said was, 'the Nova is coming home. All is well'. That gave everyone on Sol a sigh of relief. Then, Arna realized that they were coming home. They could be married. Her greatest desire would be met. She began the task of putting everything together, except for the vettig that would be officiating at the wedding. She knew that Jay wouldn't let her down about that important part of the wedding. After all, he had promised. She got everyone involved, including the Empress. She was her father's daughter. She kept barking out orders like the admiral, her father would, to everyone. She was commanding an army, and she knew it. She was going to have every thing looking perfect. So that her 'stoic warrior' could not back down from his promise. This she vowed.

"Arna, what's going on here?" Her father asked, seeing all of the commotion going on.

"We're having a wedding, whether anybody likes it or not," she replied.

"I really feel sorry for Jay. I hope he knows what he's getting into," the admiral said shaking his head.

Arna, who began to giggle over that her father. "Dad, don't be a pessimist. Besides, you know that I'm doing it for his own good."

With that the admiral turned and left the Great Hall. The Great Hall had been given to Arna for her wedding ceremony as one of the wedding gifts that the Imperial Family wanted to give her. And she was going to do just that. She was going to make this one of the most memorable weddings in the history of the Empire. This was her dream wedding. She had to do something or she would go crazy. This gave her the outlet she needed to keep her mind off things. She was glad when her mother and her future mother-in-law suggested it. And even gladder when the Emperor and the Empress agreed. She was the admiral-in-charge this time.

Back on the Nova things were running normal. The doctor had returned and the Grand Vettig had decided to ride with the captain on the Nova, his own ship following.

"Thank you, captain, for allowing me to be a passenger aboard your ship. It is a marvelous ship at that," the Grand Vettig said.

"It's a very worthy vessel," the captain replied. "I'm very fond of her."

"Captain, we need you down on space deck five," a voice that sounded like the chief engineer's said.

"What now? By your leave, Your Holiness," the captain said respectfully.

"By all means, duty calls," came the reply. The Grand Vettig was seated in the left-hand chair next to the captain's on the bridge.

The captain entered the lift and took it to the space deck mentioned. He found himself entering into a darkened area. He looked around to see if anyone was there and then called for the lights to come on. It was at that moment that a crowd of people came out and shouted hale to the captain. Then a bunch of balloons came from the high ceiling. Then they started to sing, 'for he is a jolly good fellow.' A look of embarrassment came across the captain's face.

"How did you? When did you?" The captain got out through his embarrassment.

"Well, the doctor found her way here after realizing you were okay back there on the planet. She was able to replicate the balloons and the confetti. Then she got a few of my men to hang it all up. And there you are," the chief engineer said.

"But, why?"the captain asked.

"Well, I must admit that I was a part of this. They wanted me to keep you a little occupied on the bridge, while they did this," the Grand Vettig said.

"You're, forgiven. But that doesn't answer my question," the captain said.

"Captain, this is a celebration. Twofold, one for our recent victory. Two more importantly, this is your bachelor party. Per the doctor's orders, everything is being done in good taste. And knowing who you're going to marry it is being done respectably," the XO said laughing. And the rest of the crowd laughed with him.

Everyone came to the captain and shook his hand and patted him on the back. They told stories of his conquests in battle. They told embarrassing stories about his early days as a captain of the ship, especially, the XO. And the doctor began telling my tale of the gentler side of the captain. It almost made the captain want to cry. All in all it was a good celebration.

"Captain, we've also recorded everything at this party for you and your future bride to watch sometime in the future.

We wanted to make sure, not only that you would remember us. But that it would embarrass you as well. But on a more serious note, we wanted to thank you for being who you are," the science officer said, waxing poetic.

"Speech! Speech!" The crowd yelled enthusiastically.

"Friends, and sneaky friends," the captain began as the crowd laughed. "It is I that needs to give you the thanks. You are the finest crew that anyone anywhere could ever have. And I am so proud to be your captain. But I am prouder still to call you friends. And everyone that isn't on duty, one we get back is invited to the wedding. I wanted to let you know that the past few weeks have been very tedious, but rewarding. XO, Tinker, Doctor, Hal, I want them four you to be my groomsmen. You are my closest friends, and I couldn't think of anybody else to get that distinction to," the captain said. The doctor began to cry. The men began to strut around sticking their chests out. Everyone else began to cheer again. The Grand Vettig shook the captain's hand in approval.

"What am I supposed to do as a groomsman? I've never been one before," the doctor asked. Everyone began to laugh. Even though it wasn't traditional to have a woman in that role, it was allowable. Yes, the captain had everything he wanted. But there was still something nagging at him. It seemed that everything was going too smooth. He wondered what danger was still lurking out there.

Back on Sol the army of Arna was on full maneuvers. Chairs were being set up in formation. Ribbons with her wedding colors, red and white, were being placed all over. And red and white flowers were being arranged throughout the Great Hall. And a red runner was being rolled out down the center of the chairs. In the front of the chairs, a white platform was placed. Behind the platform red curtains were hung on a frame of plastic piping. And arched trellis was placed on the stage with red roses woven throughout it. Arna stood back and surveyed the whole thing. A smile of pleasure came across her face. She said to her self, how perfect this all looks.

"Arna! Arna!" Her mother yelled to her entering the Great Hall. "We need to get to your fitting. Your dress won't be done in time, if we don't."

"Alright, Mother, I'll be right there!" She called back.

Her mother approached her and began to speak. "Arna, everything looks just fine. I'm so proud of you. You've been a real trooper," she said.

"I hope everything will be alright. I want everything to be just perfect," Arna said.

"How could it be any other way. You're marrying the man you love, as it should be. You look so happy, the happiest I've seen you look in your life. This is almost like the time we got to that horse. Remember when you were 12," her mother said.

"I remember," she said tenderly, putting her arms around her mother's neck, hugging her. Then the two turned, her mother linking arms with her, and walked out of the Great Hall to go have her fitting done. In the fitting room she tried on several different gowns, then, she found the one she wanted. It was hand woven silk, pure white, no dyes. The bottom part flowed out into a train about 4 feet long. The upper part, had a pattern similar to that of doilies on an end table with a background of white covering her completely. The dress was just the perfect one, her 'stoic warrior' would approve. It would be the perfect complement to his dress whites. Then the veil was attached to a crown of red and white scarves woven around a wire frame, showing the wedding colors. It was about that time that her father came to see where she was.

"Arna, Arna, are you in there?" The admiral said knocking on the door to the room.

"Arn, stay out. Just for a moment, please," his wife begging him.

He turned the knob and pushed open the door anyway. "What's up? I'm not the groom. And I've seen her many times in different types of dress," the admiral said.

"It's not that. She just feels self-conscious about the whole thing," his wife replied.

He looked at how beautiful she was. And a tear began to well up in his eyes. "My! Don't you look beautiful!" He said pulling out a handkerchief dabbing it on his eyes.

"Don't, Dad. You'll get me to cry, too. You make my mascara run," Arna said, going over to give her dad a hug, consoling him. "It's okay. I'm just getting married." Then she twirled around to show him a better view of her dress.

"I'm okay. I was just thinking it was only yesterday, wasn't it, Dawn, that we were just changing her diapers?" He says with a little gentility, in his voice.

"I think it was, Sweetheart," Dawn replied. They all began to smile.

"Oh, you two. You're making me blush. I love you," Arna said, giving them both a hug. Then she slugged her father on the shoulder. "If you tell that story to Jay I'll disown you. At least for a month." Then they all laughed and felt better about themselves.

"The reason why I came was to let you know that the Nova will be here tomorrow at about 0900 hours. That's 9 AM for you two," the admiral said, teasing them.

"Then we'll have to rush everything. I thought I had more time. Dad, can you help me? I mean, there's just one more thing I need," she said, being rather cryptic. "Mom, can you give us a little time to ourselves, please." Giving her a look that only mothers understood at times like these, there needed to be a little father, daughter conference. Then her mother left the room to give them privacy.

"What is it that you needed?" The admiral asked.

"Dad, I want you to walk me down the aisle," she said.

"Of course. That was my intention," he said, interrupting her.

"No. Don't interrupt me. I want you to walk me down the aisle and give me away. But, I need you after the ceremony to reserve one last dance for me. But when you give me away, don't think that you've gotten rid of me. Just think we've expanded our family," she said, finishing her speech holding back the tears.

"Sweetheart, I already think that way. Jay is a good man. And I know that he is an honorable man. And that he commands respect, respect that you had better give to him or I'll paddle your hiney. Do you understand?" The admiral said.

"Yes, I do," she replied, pouting and nodding her head in agreement. She knew that she could be a hand full for anybody. But she also knew her love for her man out weighed everything else. Theirs would be a love that could be written about in the history books. It seemed that her fairy tale romance was becoming a reality.

As advanced as the society was, there were some traditions worth keeping as far Arna and Jay thought.. Both Arna and Jay never consummated their relationship with sex. Nor had they had such relations with anybody else. They both believed in what the

Holy Chronicles spelled out, that any other behavior of this was wrong. It would have amazed the public at large. There were so many different philosophies floating around out there. But these two felt the philosophy that they opted to follow was the right one. In fact there were several auto-graphs written on the subject. Besides, the captain was too busy with his job. And Arna was busy with her education. They kept focused on the truth and the promise that they were only for one another and no one else.

On the Nova the party was winding down, when the chief communications officer, Lieut. Cmdr. Rahm spoke up. "Captain, I know that most of the gifts given to couples on this occasion are usually for the bride. But I don't think it's fair that she gets all the fun. So, we've put together a little video. We want you to watch it in your quarters tonight just before you go to bed. But be careful in my keep you awake," he said, with everyone else laughing.

"If it does. I'll hold you responsible, mister," the captain said, pointing his finger at him. Then he'll laugh right along with everybody else.

"Captain, I've a little something, also. How he knew about it I'm not quite for sure, but Colonel Parr sent a little something," the X0 said.

"Well, let's have a look," said the captain. The XO handed him a video cartridge that had been downloaded from the colonel's transmission. They had just received a transmission about two hours prior to the party. There was a notation on the outside of the cartridge that said, Congratulations, on your upcoming nuptials. This is to be seen in private.

"I'll look at it in my own quarters when this is all over," the captain said pointing around at the party. "And it looks like it's dying down already."

"And captain, I'm glad the X0 was a good little boy," the doctor says smiling. Her and her husband left hand-in-hand being one of the last ones to leave.

"Captain, may I walk with you a while?" The Grand Vettig asked.

"By all means," the captain replied, waving his hand toward the door in a manner we fashion.

"May I take a long, captain?" the XO asked.

"Sure, the more the merrier," the captain replied. With that the three walked down the corridor to the lift and took it to officer's country. They were relatively quiet on the way there. Arriving at the captain's quarters the Grand Vettig bid them a fond farewell and went on to the guest quarters.

"I'm rather curious as to what the colonel sent you. May I come in and view it with you?" The XO asked.

"Why not. I'm not really tired and I could use the company," the captain replied.

"How do you think he Knew?" The XO asked

"Who are you talking about?" The captain asked in return.

"The colonel," he replied.

"You know their intelligence as well as I do. It's pretty good," The captain said.

"Yes, I do. But we're not supposed to say anything about that," the XO said.

"We have freedom of speech. We can admire the enemy or should I say our acquaintance. If we want to. Besides, they do deserve the recognition," the captain replied.

"Well, I could use some tea. How about you?" The X0 asked. With that he went over to the food synthesizer and ordered up the tea.

They settled in to watch the video, and the captain put the cartridge in the slot and commanded the computer to play the tape. Then the tape began like this: "My dear captain, I thought you might like to hear something. My ship was given a new assignment as far away from the Titanium Barrier as possible. And we came across a very familiar type of planet. Now for the rest of the message." It was the colonel prefacing, what was to come next.

"My name is Zebub. And if you are watching this message. I'm no longer on this planet. I've escaped..."

As the message continued the captain looked at the X0 in amazement. "How many of these beings, are there?" The XO asked.

"I don't know. But, let's don't tell anybody about this one yet. I know what we need to do. And we're going to do it. I'm getting married and the crew needs a rest," the captain replied.

"I'm with you. We've had enough excitement for one day. Besides, you need to get rested for that little filly you have back home," the XO said being fatherly. And with that he left, shaking his head, realizing they had plenty of time for the next adventure.

On the Star Blaster the colonel was smiling to himself. He figured it was just about now that the Captain of the Nova was watching his little gift. The one thing he didn't say was that he knew who this rogue vettig was. He had seen him with the Prime Minister when making his initial report about the other rogue vettigs, just a few days before. He had been given this assignment because of his involvement in the whole thing. This was his punishment and a way for the Prime Minister to keep a handle on him. This region of space was considered the

Badlands. And nobody wanted to go to the Badlands. But the colonel knew that it would only be a matter of time before he was back in good graces with the Prime Minister. Or at least one of his cabinet members that would speak on his behalf to the Prime Minister.

It was about 0700 hrs., that the captain woke up and went to the officer's mess. He found the Grand Vettig, already there. He looked like that he was enjoying a cup of tea. The captain ordered his breakfast and went over to sit with the Grand Vettig.

"Captain, how are you doing this fine morning?" The Grand Vettig asked.

"I'm doing just fine. But I would like to talk to you about something. Can we keep it confidential, I mean, between you and me?" The captain asked.

"We vettigs take the confidentiality of the confessional sacred. So, talk away," the Grand Vettig said smiling.

"You remember last night? When I got that present from the colonel," the captain asked.

"Why, yes I do," he replied.

"I thought about it all night and figured I needed to say something to you. It was all about another bad guy named Zebub. You know what I mean," the captain said, winking at him.

"Captain, don't worry about it at this time. We've all the time in the universe to catch him. We've had a victory just recently. He won't be lashing out at us anytime soon. So, go ahead with your plans. We need something positive to happen to boost the morale of the Empire and the Emperor," the Grand Vettig replied comforting him.

"I don't care what anybody says, you're all right in my book. If you make a good human being. If you know what I mean," the captain replied again, winking at him. The Grand Vettig just laughed. And took it as a compliment in the manner in which it was given. He was growing to like the captain. He was glad that he agreed to officiate his wedding.

Then there was a call to the captain to come to the bridge. They were just a few minutes away from Sol. The captain left orders to call him when that happened. The captain went over to the bulkhead that had the communication panel on it, and flipped the button. "I'll be on the bridge, momentarily. When we get to Sol set up a standard orbit, in accordance with Central Command's specifications. Is that understood?" The captain said.

"Aye! Aye! Captain," came the reply from the helmsman.

The captain went back to the table to sit down and continue his conversation with the Grand Vettig. "As I was saying, you're my type of guy. And I'm glad that I was able to unload this burden," the captain said.

"Captain, that's quite all right. Sometimes, people don't understand the necessity of doing things with the right priority. But you have your priorities straight," the Grand Vettig said. "It wouldn't have done you any good to keep this a secret. Now that we know we can focus our efforts in the proper direction. If you understand what I'm trying to say there is more than your vessel out there that can help. You've done enough."

"Thank you, Your Holiness," the captain said. And with that he went to the bridge to take his rightful place as the ship's commander.

On the bridge, everything was running like clockwork. Everybody knew their place and what needed to be done as it should be. The captain was quite pleased with everyone on a job well done. Sometimes, a person just has to allow fate to take its course, he thought. And I didn't know, if we would come out of this unscathed. But then his thoughts turned toward home, and his loved ones. He thought to himself, I'm probably thinking the same way as everyone else.

As the Nova was entering orbit, there was another type of interrogation going on in the admiral's office. "Dad, what is it that Jay has to go through before I can have him?" Arna asked.

"Well, there will be a debriefing. Then there will be a ceremony of sorts. The Emperor, and the Grand Vettig both want to pin a medal on him. The debriefing will probably take a couple of hours. Then all the pomp and circumstance of the medal pinning ceremony that will be a couple more hours. Then a few questions from the Information Bureau to be broadcast throughout the empire. Then you can have him, that will take about a total of six hours. Is that all right with you?" The admiral explained.

"I guess it'll have to be," she replied, pouting.

"Sweetheart, because you're his fiancée, you'll need to be with him throughout all of this. You'll be by his side the whole time," he said consoling her.

"That's right," she said, her eyes lighting up. She realized that he wouldn't be out of her sight one moment. He was delighted at the prospect. The only time they would be out of her sight was when they were dressing for the wedding. Then she decided that she would send her father to stand guard over him until after the wedding. She giggled to herself.

The shuttle with the captain, the XO, the chief engineer, chief science officer, the doctor, and the Grand Vettig landed on the surface first. The navigator was left in charge of the Nova.

Everyone was relatively quiet on the way down. The captain was trying to figure out exactly what he would say in the debriefing. "Your Holiness, I'm glad you're with us. And I hope this doesn't take long for obvious reasons," the captain said.

"It'll take as long as it takes," the Grand Vettig replied. Everyone was amazed at his patience.

As the shuttle landed and the tail end of it opened up to a lower its passengers to disembark. There were people there already waiting on their loved ones. It was similar to the scene. When this all started. But this seemed a little bit better than that. The captain had received a communiqué from the Emperor, stating that they would be having a medal-pinning ceremony after the debriefing. The captain said to himself. This is going to take longer than what everybody thinks. They found themselves winding around the court orders of the Military Citadel to a briefing/interrogating area. There were several security personnel that met them in the corridors along the way. They were there to escort and protect as the commander in charge stated to them. They entered into the briefing area, and there sat the admiral and the joint Chiefs of Staff. Everyone knew that this was not the typical the briefing as they entered. The scene with several chairs positioned in the middle of the room facing a panel of the joint Chiefs sitting behind a table. "Gentlemen and lady, have a seat," the admiral requested.

"Admiral and honored sirs, permit me to introduce to you the Grand Vettig," the captain said.

With that the joint Chiefs stood to attention.

"Let's not stand on ceremony," the Grand Vettig replied to their salutes. "We're here for you, nothing else." Everyone was taken with his humility. But they figured that was the type of person he was due to his position.

Then the captain began the rigorous details of his mission. A majority of the joint Chiefs listened as if he were telling them a fairy tale. Everyone with the captain read it on their faces. They were quite for sure about anything other than the moon blowing up at what is now called space zero. They had heard that the Cabal Union seem to be a part of this whole mess. But even that seemed like a fairy tale the captain presented it. Then the most amazing thing happened. The Grand Vettig stood up. "Gentlemen, if you'll look on me. You'll understand more. I've been given the permission to do this," he said. With that, his whole countenance changed. They no longer saw a flesh and blood image, but rather a bright light that had a configuration similar to that of a man. They solve, what looked like a body, arms and legs, ahead, and eyes and a mouth that smiled. And if they did not think themselves to be men, they would've fainted. Then as quickly as the Grand Vettig and changed into this creature of light he went back to his original state.

"Admiral, what is it that we've just seen?" Admiral Man asked. He was the chief educational officer for the fleet.

"I'm not quite for sure," Admiral Nal replied. He was trying to figure out himself what was going on. Everyone but the captain and 'the brain trust' was amazed. In fact, he chief engineer kind of chuckled to himself over the ludicrous nature of whole thing.

"As you see, gentlemen, the captain is not mad. He is telling you the truth. The Grand Designer allowed me to show you my real self. But, through a mutual understanding with your Emperor we have decided to allow you, the joint Chiefs to know. Also, we are telling the commanding officers of all military spacecraft," the Grand Vettig explained.

"That might undermine our whole infrastructure. Don't you think?" Admiral Sil inquired.

"Well, gentlemen, we're under orders, Imperial orders to do so," Admiral Nal replied. This gave credence to what he was saying.

"We'll need time to digest all this," Admiral Man said.

"Take all the time in the world. It won't change the Emperor's mind. We must comply," Admiral Nal replied. "Gentlemen and lady, I believe that our debriefing is over. Now we are to go out to the palace lawn for the ceremony."

Then everybody left together. The joint Chiefs hung back a little ways from the others. The captain and his 'brain trust' were so used to things by now that it didn't make any difference whether they were walking with the Grand Vettig or not. The others were a little leery about the whole. Admiral Nal was walking beside Captain Gos. He was fulfilling his role as security guard per the order of his daughter. But he had been informed by the Emperor about the Grand Vettig ahead of time. So, there was no odd feelings as far as he was concerned.

As they walked out on the steps in front of the main palace. They saw a podium at the bottom of the steps. Several microphones were hooked up giving it an air of tradition. And there were several chairs placed in a semi circle fashion about three rows thick. In the front row, the parents of the captain, Arna, the XO's wife, the chief engineer's sister, and a close colleague of the Kings were seated. Behind them were several of the crew of the Nova and then behind them were several reporters.

"This is the Imperial Information Bureau coming to you live from the Palace lawn. There has been a rather interesting development, at this time. One of our very own is being given the distinguished Valor of Peacetime medal. Two things that make this unique are the last time this was given was over 500 years ago. Then it was given to, an ancestor of Admiral Nal, the chief of Space Operations. It was given to him for his work in civil rights. If you'll remember your history correctly, he was the one that led the Peaceable Revolution. We're all excited today. The second unique thing is that not only is it being given to the captain of the Nova. But it is also being given to the entire crew of the Nova. The captain will be the representative for the crew in receiving this distinguished honor. Cal, let's take a look at what's happening right now," the reporter, Cor Men, said. With that the camera panned down to the Palace Lawn. The Emperor had not come on the scene yet. "As you can see, the captain and his entourage have arrived. They are waiting on the Emperor as we speak. I believe the Emperor has to feel very honored at this time. Don't you think, Cyn?"

"Well, Cor, it is an amazing site to see. We have been told by the Bureau that for matters of Imperial security they cannot tell us why this medal is being given," Cyn said.

"But, Cyn, we have been told that the captain and his crew faced imminent danger to keep the peace. We were also told that there was the possibility of an interstellar war. But work kind of unclear as to with whom," Cor said. "I see that the Emperor and the Empress have arrived."

"And isn't she looking lovely in her dress. I'm told it is a one-of-a-kind done for her by the designer, Dra Ma," Cyn said.

"Yes, she is. And the Emperor is looking rather dashing, himself," Cor replied. "The Emperor is about to speak. Let's listen." And they turned toward the Emperor.

"I'm, pleased, that you could all come out to this auspicious occasion. I am told that this is being simulcast throughout the empire. It has been over 500 years since we have given this commendation to anyone. Let alone to an entire crew. This medal is the highest we can give during peacetime. And it gives us pleasure to be stowed this honor upon you, Captain Gos. We honor you and the crew of the Nova with the distinguished Medal of Valor Cross. This is for your distinguished service to the empire in averting war. And we wish to present this to you at this time. Along with this medal, you will receive a letter of commendation in your service record. There will be letters of commendation, and other authentic medals given to your crew," the Emperor said. With that he pinned the medal on the captain's lapel. And applause came from, everyone there.

"This is an auspicious occasion. The Medal of Valor is a very high honor indeed. Cal, and show our audience what that medal looks like," Cor said. With that the images segued to a close-up of the medal. What the audience saw was a cross with a gentle bird perched in the center

holding a banner with the words valor and peace printed on it. This was placed on on a highly polished white pearl background, then trimmed in gold. Then there were multicolored ribbons attached to a pinning mechanism. The audience of the Information Bureau, must have been in awe of the sight.

"Cor, there is meaning in every detail of this medal. The cross which looks like a plus sign is actually a cross road, meaning that you have choices to make. The gentle bird is a symbol of peace. The banner emphasizes courage during peacetime. The white pearl background is also a symbol of peace, representing the ancient flags of truce. The gold symbolizes the richness that peacetime affords," Cyn explained.

"Yes, and a little more about the flags of truce. If you'll remember your history, these flags of truce were used to allow a peaceful exchange between warring factions," Cor intervened. "And today we see how honored everyone is."

"And, Cor, we are told that after this ceremony that there will be another one that is just as auspicious. It seems that the honored captain is getting married," Cyn said.

"That's right. If you'll look in the front row from left to right. You will see first, the captain's father and mother, then next to his mother, his fiancée. Isn't she lovely," Cor said. As the camera concentrated on the first row of chairs.

"Yes, she is. We have been told that we are welcomed at the ceremony. But we will not be making any commentary during the ceremony. That commentary will happen after at the reception," Cyn said. "This is to allow our audience to enjoy the occasion."

CHAPTER 12

As the ceremony on the Palace lawn came to an end, everybody went inside to begin the wedding ceremony. Arna rushed as quickly as he could so Jay didn't have a chance to see her. Her father and the 'brain trust' whisked away Jay. He didn't even have time to say anything to anybody. "Jay, we need you to stay in this room here until we're ready for you. Do you understand?" The admiral said.

"I understand. I wish I could've had time to see Arna," he replied.

"In the rest of you keep him here. That's an order," the admiral said pointing at each and everyone of them.

Everyone began to laugh at the captain. Tanker, the chief engineer stood guard at the door. "You'll have to get by me, if you can," he said pointing at his chest with his thumb.

"I'll stay put," the captain replied. The room that they occupied had several chairs. So, the captain sat down. "My friends, a term I use loosely right now." He laughed. "But seriously, I have to tell you something."

"Don't start getting mushy on us, Sonny," the XO said.

"No. I mean something else. Pappy, I need to tell everyone else, what we saw last night," the captain said.

"If you think that's necessary. Go ahead," the XO replied.

"Well, the gift that we were given from the colonel wasn't what we thought it was," the captain started pointing at the XO and himself. "There's another one of those crazy characters running around out there, still. His name is Zebub. He's just like the other two we captured. But, Pappy, I didn't tell you this part. I told the Grand Vettig."

"What did he say?" The XO asked.

"He said go ahead with the days festivities. But something keeps nagging at me," he said.

"What's that?" The doctor asked.

"That's this, where is he? And what is he up to? Something doesn't seem right about this whole thing. Why would they Grand Vettig be so eager to let him go?" The captain pointed out.

"Well, from my observations he knows what he's doing. Besides, we need to have a little breather. Let's deal with it as it comes," the pragmatist, Hal said.

"That's sound advice, captain," the chief engineer said.

"But, Tinker, you don't understand. I think he's closer than we think," the captain said, still uneasy.

"Like I said, we'll deal with it as it comes," Hal said again.

In another part of the building in a low but more spacious room Arna was getting dressed. Her mother and her mother-in-law-to-be were in attendance. She put on the dress, her mother is it that the back end of it, and her mother-in-law-to-be pulled the the train around in order for it to be behind her. Then the two older women looked at her, and both began sobbing. "Stop. You two will give me doing that. And I don't want to have to fix my face all over again," Arna said.

"But you look so beautiful," her mother replied, sobbing into a hanky.

"She does look beautiful. And, Arna, welcome to the family," Jay's mother said, hugging her.

"Thank you, Mother Gos. And don't you start crying, or I will have to straighten up my face. And that'll take an extra 10 minutes," Arna told her.

In the Great Hall people were wandering in. Ushers were seating people. The way the church were configured the thrones were perpendicular to them being set on the right-hand side of everyone according to the book of protocols. Once everyone had their seats, then the Emperor and Empress would enter and be seated. Stationed throughout the Great Hall were Imperial guards as a precautionary measure. Everyone that came in were in awe of the decorations. They saw all the color scheme of red and white, and how they complemented each other. There were large, red and white bows hanging from the ceiling, red and white balloons, sticking on freestanding stands, in the first two rows had been red and white bows on them indicating these were family and close friend's seating. Many thought that they were attending a royal wedding in stead of a commoner's wedding. But many that were there had been watching the Information Bureau's broadcast that just happened, and realized why such a thing was happening. There was a stage set up so that all could see with the arched trellis, curtain backdrop, and the wedding colors very prevalent throughout. At this point it looked relatively bare having no one on the stage. The cameras for the Information Bureau were running and the reporters were seated appropriately.

"It all looks so marvelous, doesn't it?" Mana Niel, Dar Niel's wife said. Dar being Pappy, the XO.

"It sure does," came the reply of the elder Mr. Gos. Who is seated nearby.

As the Great Hall was filling up out of nowhere, there seemed to be a little maneuvering on the stage. The Grand Vettig had taken his place, along with the captain and his groomsmen. The vettig, had his official royal wedding garb on, the captain and his entourage were in dress whites. The vettig's royal wedding garb was a robe with red, purple, blue, and white. On his head was what was called the Great Crown of the Grand Designer. The Crown had similar colors, but in the middle just above the four head was a red cross looking like a plus sign against a background of white. The group on the stage was very anxious having to wait on the proceedings to begin.

"Captain, we're all behind you. And Sonny, if you mess this up. I'll be the first one in line to get you," the XO said.

"Pappy, if I mess this up. I'll let you," the captain replied. And the others kind of chuckled to themselves, knowing that the XO was teasing. He was trying to add to the anxiety that the captain felt. It was his way of getting revenge on the captain. Because the captain had done the same thing to him at his wedding.

The tension was so thick you could cut it with a knife. It was only superseded by the thought of getting married. The captain stood there looking dumbfounded as most potential grooms did it this time. The admiral shook his head as if to say, I hope he knows what he's doing. The admiral's wife was crying and dabbing her face with a handkerchief. The captain's father was beaming with pride. And his mother was following suit with the admiral's wife by crying and using a handkerchief in the same way. His younger brother was sitting beside his mother, giving the looks. And next to him was the XO's wife. Then there were a couple of close friends, from his early days at the Imperial Fleet Academy. With the admiral and his wife was Arna's cousin. Next to her was her cousin's parents. And next to them was a couple of close friends from college. As the camera was showing the crowd as it honed in on the crowd it showed names under the individuals in the front rows. This was so that everybody could tell who the families were and who the friends were, in contrast with the crowd. Then, the wedding march played as each of the bridesmaids started down the red runner going down the middle of the chair to the stage. Then that all too familiar refrain was played on the organ to announce the bride. The crowd stood to their feet, some smiling, and some in awe. As Arna proceeded to the stage. The captain thought to himself, I'm a very fortunate man. Besides the beautiful dress, and the veil with the red and white ground aborning her, she held a bouquet of red and white roses. As she arrived at the side of her groom-to-be she took her place at his left side. The left side was considered the love side, because the heart was on the that side.

"Friends and neighbors, family members, we are here today on this auspicious occasion to see these two come together in the bonds of holy matrimony. It has been my pleasure to get to know Captain Gos over the last few days. And I am privileged to be officiating this wedding. Holy matrimony is an institution not taken lightly. It has been a tradition handed down since the first wedding ceremony was instituted by the Grand Designer. And we are assembled here today to unite Captain Jay Gos and Arna Nal in the bonds of holy matrimony. The Holy

Chronicles teaches that it is the gift of the Grand Designer. And that it is a commitment which one man and one woman make to each other and to Him. Jay and Arna, will you now join your right hands together to make the following vows. Who gives this woman to be married?" the Grand Vettig said. And with that, they joined each other's hands, as directed and waited for the answer to the question.

"Her mother, and I do," the admiral answered and then seated himself.

"Jay, will you take Arna to be your lawful wedded wife, and will you promise to love, honor, support, and treat her with dignity, keeping only to her, as long as you both live?" The Grand Vettig said, facing the captain.

"I will," the captain replied.

"Arna, will you take Jay to be your lawful wedded husband, and will you promise to love, honor, support, and treat him with dignity, keeping only to him, as long as you both live?" The Grand Vettig said, facing Arna.

"I will," she replied.

"A home is built on love, which is a virtue that is portrayed in the 10th chapter of the Epistle of Love which says, love is patient and kind, love is not jealous or boastful, it is not arrogant or rude. Love does not insist on its own way, it is not irritable or resentful, it doesn't rejoice at wrong, but rejoices in the right. Love tries to do everything in the right way with the right attitude. Love bears all things, believes all things, hopes all things, endures all things. Love never ends. Love never fails. So faith, hope, and love abide, these three; but the greatest of these is love.

Marriage is a companionship, a journey filled with hope, and is one of the greatest institutions ever given to man.

Marriage involves mutual commitment and responsibility. And affords some of the greatest joys of life. When two agreed to share their lives in this most holy of institutions. They agree to share in the sorrows, in the joys, and the mundane things of day-to-day living.

You are exhorted to dedicate your home and your lives to the Grand Designer and His message. Taking His message to any and all that will listen. Using the Holy Chronicles as your guide.

Let us pray. O Grand Designer of life and love, bestowed your Grace upon this marriage, and seal this commitment of your children with your law.

As you have brought them together by your divine design, sanctify them by your Spirit, that they may give themselves fully, one to the other and to you. In the name of thy Holy Child, Amen.

Who has the wedding bracelets?" The vettig pronounced.

"I do," the XO said being the best man.

"The wedding bracelet is a symbol of two binding themselves together as one. It is made of a pure silk, with threads of gold spun within it. The silk is a pure white symbolizing purity of heart. The gold is symbolic of the richness that marriage towards the couple. As they placed these around each other's wrists they are making a vow to bind themselves to one another to become one. This is a bond of string, that cannot be broken. Will you take these tokens and bind them to one another's left wrist," the vettig said. And with that, they did as directed . The left wrist, signifying a never ending love for one another.

"Jay , will you give this bracelet and repeat after me, Arna, with this bracelet, I pledge my life and my love to you in the name of the Grand Designer and his son," Jay repeated what the vettig had said.

"Arna, will you give this bracelet and repeat after me, Jay, with disparate bracelet, I pledge my life and my love to you in the name of the Grand Designer and his son," Arna repeated what the vettig had said.

"Will you both please repeat after me: Entreat me not to leave you or to return from following you; for where you go, I will go, and where you lodge, I will lodge; and your people shall be my people, and your God my God," the two of them repeated what the vettig had said.

"Since they have made these commitments before the Grand Designer and this assembly, by the authority given to me in their site, I now pronounce you man and wife. And what has been joined together let no man put asunder," the vettig said. "Face the crowd," he whispered to them. "Let me present to you, Captain and Mrs. Gos. You may kiss your bride." With that crowd stood up applauding, and Jay enthusiastically grabbed Arna and kissed her.

After the kiss they ran down the aisle to the door. Then the crowd led by the bridesmaids and groomsmen. At the door everyone was handed a bag of biodegradable confetti, one of the marvels of technology, whereby the confetti, would these all into the ground as harmless chemicals compatible with nature. They began to throw the confetti at them as a matter of tradition. The happy couple made their way to the Royal limo that had been decorated with a sign that said, just married, several ropes were tied to its bumper with shoes attached spaced about every foot or so, and a large part was painted in its rear window with water washable paint. The shoes dragged behind the car, to say we are speeding you on your way in your new life. Everyone was laughing and having a great time of it all. The captain and his bride, would drive around for you while to announce to the world their nuptials. Then they would be going back to the Grand Ballroom of the Palace for their reception.

"Sweetheart, I'm most fortunate of all men. You don't know how much this means to me, do you?" Jay said with tears in his eyes.

"You don't know how much this means to me," she said, also with tears in her eyes. She realized that this was the first time she had seen him cry. Then she remembered a story, her mother told her one time about a good friend of hers she met in college. Her mother had told her how this friend had another friend in college. That they played together, laughed together, and dated together. One day, the friend left. A few years later, her mother asked her friend, whatever happened to so-and-so? Her friend replied to her mother at the time, 'who?' Then her mother explained about the playing, laughing, and dating. She replied, 'oh her! Well, she's not, you.' Then her mother further explained what she meant. She told her that they laughed together, played together, and dated together but they had never cried together. Her mother realized at that time what a good friend, she had. Because of that, right at that moment Arna realized her good fortune with Jay.

After a couple of hours driving around the happy couple headed back to the Grand Ballroom of the Palace. Having been driven around with little is happy rituals like couples have done for many years. A tradition that gave much pleasure to them. And give them a chance to talk to one another in a very intimate setting.

As they entered into the Grand Ballroom of the Palace crowd turned and began to applaud. The captain was handed a glass of synthetic champagne. And the bride was handed a bouquet to her later on during the festivities. The original bouquet was still in the limo. Then they were ushered to their table. Where they were greeted by their parents and wedding party. As they joined them, they had big smiles on their faces. "Captain, be seated. That's an order," the XO said.

"Watch yourself," the captain said, pointing at the XO.

"Captain, is everything going okay? I mean, have your nerves calmed?" The doctor asked.

"What are you talking about, doctor? He's happy. Aren't you, darling?" Arna replied.

You could tell that he was a little nervous. But it wasn't about the day's festivities. He couldn't shake that feeling that something was going to happen. He couldn't quite put his finger on it. But he was the happiest he had been in a long time. "Tinker, when we get back, make sure you calibrate our sensors," he commented.

"Sweetheart, no shoptalk. Okay?" Arna said, slapping him on the shoulder. She figured that she would get enough of that on board ship after the honeymoon. Jay just chuckled.

"As you all know, we are here because somebody got brave," the XO said, giving a speech while everyone else laughed. "I don't know which one was braver, the captain or the bride." There was even more laughing after the statement. "But seriously, there have never been two more suited for each other. The captain, I have known for while, and I have gotten to know are fairly well, and I just want to say congratulations. So, everyone, lift your glasses and toast the happy couple." And everybody followed his direction, lifting their glasses and saluting the happy couple.

"I guess it's my turn. When I was asked to be one of the groomsmen. I chuckled to myself. Because, I didn't know what a groomsmen did," the doctor said, gaining a greater laugh when the XO. "But, I took on this nontraditional role, at least for me, because I wanted to be a part of a wonderful adventure. That adventure, being the journey of wedded bliss. Now, when I first heard about their engagement. I wondered if they'd ever argued with one another. My reasoning is very simple, if you can argue with one another and still be together, that's love. But looking at the happy couple. I think that they have. Here's to you." She lifted her glass and imbibed in the drink to salute the happy couple. "Oh! I think the baby kicked." Then everyone applauded, not only for the speech before the quaint way she announced her pregnancy.

"Well, I guess I need equal time," Hal, the doctor's husband said. "Because, my wife has let the proverbial cat out of the bag. I wish to thank everyone for all their support. But this isn't our day. This is your day. You'll have plenty of time to think about kids in the future. And it doesn't make any difference how intelligent you are having a baby can make you an emotional wreck. So, take your time and get to know one another." He lifted his glass to salute the happy couple is well. And everyone around them, all laughed and giggled about his honesty.

"I guess it's my turn. I just want to say, which cousin is it that you want to do interviews me to?" Tinker said. Everyone really began to laugh at this time. And the cousin he was talking about began to blush.

"Being the father of the bride and the one who had to put up with this whole thing, it's my turn. When I first realized how serious my daughter was about you, I shook my head. When I realized you were serious about her, I shook my head. When you told me in the limo, a few weeks ago, you were going to propose, I shook my head. And when she was wandering around here like the admiral-in-charge, I shook my head. But seeing the two of you together, I still shake my head. But my heart, nods in approval of a man that has honor, integrity, and my support," the admiral said. Tears were rolling down on his face and the captain was blushing as he stood to shake the admiral's hand. Then the admiral turned to his daughter and gave her a big hug. "Save a dance for me, honey."

She nodded to him in agreement. "Arna, I love you. That's all I can say right now," her mother said, sobbing. And then she went to her and began to hug her neck.

"Arna, I love you, too. You're a part of this family, now," Jay's mother said. And mimicked Arna's mother.

"I guess I'm the last of the crowd. So that must make me the best. When Jay told me I was his plans to marry Arna, I was pleased. Not only were we gaining a daughter, we were gaining good friends. Her father and I met each other many years ago. It was when Jay was in the Academy. The admiral was there on one of his inspection tours. I saw a man of great character. He was somebody I would have followed into battle. He just had that bearing about himself. He commanded respect. It'd only been a few years prior that I heard his speech on Equality of Men. And having seen them in person, I felt awe. Then when I met his daughter I fell in love. And if I wasn't married at the time, she would've been the one," Jay's father said. The Jay's mother belted him on the shoulder, and then laughed. "But seriously, I'm happy that not only is my son happy, but so is his bride." Just about that time there was a commotion right in front of the head table. Out of nowhere, seemingly, a figure appeared.

"There is no need for alarm. My name's Zebub. And I'm here for the captain. Where is he?" The vettig said.

"I'm right here," the captain replied, standing up.

"You think you're so smug. Standing there, all dressed up. You would think that you were at a wedding," he laughed maniacally and looking around.

"What do you want?" The captain asked, taking charge.

"I want what anybody wants, power. But I'll settle for revenge," he replied gritting his teeth.

Just about that timing, everything froze. It wasn't that everyone was frozen from their but it

seemed like time was frozen. Only the captain and the vettig were mobile. The captain looked around realizing this, and lunged at the vettig. He wrestled him to the floor, knocking the weapon it was wielding out of his hand. It was just like before, on Beil's planet. The captain got him in an arm-lock and held them there. Then everyone came out of their time freeze. They all saw the same thing. They saw the captain had everything well in hand. Then, to vettigs came to the captain's aid, relieving him of Zebub.

"Everyone, stay calm. We have everything well in hand. This is something that is on a need to know basis. So, stay calm," the captain said. He then turned to see the Grand Vettig approach.

"Again, we give you our thanks. We knew that he may try something, but you're in no danger," he said.

"Did you see what happened? I mean about that time freeze," the captain asked.

"I told you before, captain, that you have somebody helping you," he replied pointing upward. "But this time I saw what you meant. I was allowed to glimpse at what I can only say is pure love. The Grand Designer has been watching."

"I'm glad he was," the captain replied.

"Captain, I didn't even see you move. You must be faster than Tinker," the XO said, having seen Tinker in a martial arts match.

"When we have time, Pappy, I'll tell you what really happened. I'm not quite for sure, if I understand it all," the captain replied.

"Sweetheart, are you okay?" Arna said rushing to his side.

"Yes, I am, Honey," he replied. Then he kissed her in the crowd said, ahh! "Let's go on with the festivities!" He turned to his bride, and asked her for a dance. She nodded her head, and then they began to dance. The little hairs on the back of his neck had calmed themselves.

Everything was all right with the world. After the captain and his bride began to dance. Then others followed suit, first the doctor and her husband, then the admiral and his wife, and Jay's parents came next. Then the dance floor filled up.

After the first dance, the Grand Vettig stood in the midst of her one and said, "I want to bless the happy couple. Would you bow your heads in reverence, as I pray." He then laid his hands on their heads, respectively. "We ask that you bless this happy couple, oh Grand Designer. Let them have a wonderful life, a wonderful romance, and a lot of love for one another. Allow that their kids be brought up in the admonition of love and your holy word. In the name of thy Holy Son, Amen." Then everyone lifted their heads and went back to the festivities. The grand that it shook the hand of the captain and patted the forehead of his bride. Then he left. As he did, he said to himself, "we'll keep in touch. You have many adventures ahead of you. And you're very important to the Grand Designer."

EPILOGUE

The science director had left the Grand Ballroom having forgotten his gift for the happy couple. As he found himself wandering through the halls heading to his office he spied one of the many offices of the science directory, open. He ducked his head in to see what was going on. "Gentlemen, what are you doing here?" He asked, seeing two of his colleagues seated in front of a communication panel. One of them had earphones listening to some sort of message.

"Doctor Miah. You startled us," Professor Rain replied.

"That doesn't answer my question, gentlemen," the science director, Jer Miah said.

"You need to hear this," the other professor said offering the headphones to him.

"What am I listening to?" He asked.

"This is a message that one of our deep space probes, captured and relayed back to us. It's very interesting. You really need to listen," he said. With that the Science Director put on the headphones. He listened for about 15 to 20 minutes.

"I need to tell the Emperor about this," the science director replied.

Then the science director left the office and rushed to see the Emperor. Professor Rain looked at his colleague, puzzled. His colleague, Professor Bo said, listen to this. Then he switched the knob on the console to cause the original message to come over the speakers of the communication panel.

"We have a situation here. It is a situation that has been designed by God. You're not here by chance, but by design. You see a long time ago, God in his infinite wisdom, had a plan for us. He wanted us to be where he is, Heaven. Heaven is a kingdom of light, a kingdom of life, and a kingdom full of love. He sent His Son to die in our place. He went through an agonizing death. He was betrayed by one of his own with a kiss. He was tried in a kangaroo court. This was a trial, full of inconsistencies. He was mocked. He was beaten. He was scourged. The Bible says, by his stripes we are healed. He was then taken to Golgotha's Hill to be crucified. Crucifixion was for the worst criminals of the day. It caused one to have his lungs collapse as he had his arms stretched out and nailed to that cross. They spit on him, they pull his beard out, and he did not look human. When they lifted him up on the cross and dropped it into a hole it jerked every fiber of his body. As he hung between heaven and earth, He spoke some of the greatest words ever spoken. He said, Father, forgive them for they know not what they do. He was thinking of you and me when he said that. With his dying breath, he asked the Father, why have you forsaken me? Then he collapsed, dead. But folks that's not the whole story. On the third day he rose from the dead. He showed everybody how true his words were, when he said, I lay down my life and I can pick it back up, at will. So my friends, if you want to be a part of this plan. I ask everyone to come forward, to give their lives to the Lord."

"My word, by the Grand Designer. What are we hearing?" Professor Bo asked pausing the recording.

"That's not all. He has to finish," he said, resuming the recording that the other professor had paused.

"Everyone up front, come closer. Give everybody room. What we are going to do next is to say a prayer. But I want to explain something to you in John 3: 16. We read, 'For God so loved the world that he gave his only begotten son, that whosoever will, could have ever lasting life.' And in Romans 10:9 and 10. It says,' if you will confess with your mouth, and believe in your heart that Jesus is Lord, you shall be saved.' Now, let me explain to you this, that if you truthfully believe in your heart. What we are about to say in our prayer. You will be saved. Now repeat after me:

> Dear Jesus...
> I am a sinner...
> and I need you...
> come into my heart...
> make me a new creature...
> I believe you came in the flesh...
> I believe you were of a virgin birth...
> that you died...
> that you rose again...
> that you ascended on high...
> and that you are forever making intercession...
> for me...
> so come into my heart...
> I pray...
> in your holy name...
> Jesus...
> Amen...

My friends, if you really believed in your heart what you just prayed your saved. The Angels, beings of light are rejoicing in your salvation.

"That was awesome," Professor Bo said. "Now, I know why, Doctor Miah was in such a hurry."

"If I know him. He'll talk, the Emperor into doing something. But it may be futile," Professor Rain said.

"What do you mean?" The other professor asked.

"Well, if the calculations are right. And I believe that they are. It means that this message came from deep space. In fact, it came from so deep into space that we could not pinpoint the exact location of its origin. All I can tell you is that it is indicative of the old radio transmissions we used to use. I mean, we used to use them about 500 years ago. And if saw me. I gave the good doctor the report before he left," he explained.

"Yes I did. In fact, he took it with him. He probably wanted to show the Emperor," he replied. "I understand, you couldn't pinpoint the exact location. What do we have a general location?"

"That we have," replied Professor Rain.

"This may open up a form new era for us," Professor Bo said.

In the Grand Ballroom of the Palace. The science director found the Emperor. "Sire! Sire! I have something I need to speak to you about. And it isn't about a moon exploding this time," the science director said.

The End or may be, it is just the Beginning.